# I only said I didn't want you because I was terrified

By Dr. Celia Banting

WIGHITA PRESS

Requests for permission to make copies of any part of the work should be mailed to the following address:

Wighita Press
P.O. Box 30399
Little Rock, Arkansas, 72260-0399

www.wighitapress.com

Library of Congress Cataloging-in-Publication Data

Banting, Celia
I Only Said I Didn't Want You Because I Was Terrified/
Dr. Celia Banting – 1st Edition
p. cm.
ISBN 0-9786648-3-3 (paperback)

1. Therapeutic novel   2. Suicide prevention   3. Teenage pregnancy
4. Trust issues

Library of Congress Control Number: 2006928592

Layout by Michelle VanGeest
Cover production by Luke Johnson

Printed by Dickinson Press, Grand Rapids, Michigan, USA

**Issues addressed in this book:**

Suicide prevention

Lying

Peer pressure

The consequences of drinking alcohol

Consensual sex

Vicarious living

Injustice and powerlessness

Signs and symptoms of pregnancy

Fetal development

Abortion

The process of birth

Early neonatal care

Avoiding maternal and infant distress

Breast feeding

Problem solving skills – reaching out to others

Repairing broken trust

Honest communication

Acceptance

## Also by Dr. Celia Banting...

*I Only Said I Had No Choice*

*I Only Said "Yes" So That They'd Like Me*

*I Only Said I Couldn't Cope*

*I Only Said I Was Telling the Truth*

• • • •

## Available after April 2007...

*I Only Said I Wanted To Kill Myself; I Didn't Really Mean It*

*I Only Said I Wasn't Hungry*

*I Only Said It Didn't Hurt*

*I Only Said I Could Handle It, But I Was Wrong*

*I Only Said Leave Me Out of It*

*Dedicated to Erica Elsie,*
*and all teenage mothers who struggle to do the right thing*

# Acknowledgments

My grateful thanks go to my proofreader and typesetter, Michelle VanGeest, who frees me from my dyslexic brain, and replaces my mother's voice. Thanks to Bev, my stray-word spotter, too. I thank my dear brother, Steve, for his computer expertise, and my wonderful husband, Des, for the inspiration and support he gives me. Thank you to Luke and Sam for their faith, inspiration and talent. Thank you to my dear friend Vicki for her guiding sense of style.

Thank you to all my psychotherapy tutors and colleagues at the Metanoia Institute, London, for teaching me about human nature, psychopathology, growth and recovery.

I thank the good Lord for giving me a lively imagination, and I also thank my parents for moving to the Isle of Wight, "the land that bobs in and out of view, depending upon the sea mist."

# Chapter One

I can't help it. Watching a bride walking down the aisle always makes me cry, and today is no exception. She looks beautiful even if she is six months pregnant. I smile at my cousin, Jade, as she walks past me, hanging on my uncle's arm, and she grins at me. I can feel my mom stiffen beside me, and I catch a glance between her and my dad that reflects everything they've been saying about Jade over the past three months. I pray the rest of the family didn't see it.

My family is a dynasty, one where everyone seems to be fighting and picking fault with each other. It's never peaceful; there's always a conflict brewing like the threat of an earth tremor, or else it's a full-blown earthquake where one side of the family is severed and split apart until time or another crisis repairs the damage.

Dad calls our family a "menagerie," a circus full of weird people, which seems a bit unkind to me but that's what he calls it. I look around the church. Sitting in the pews are cousins who I haven't seen for years and whose names I can't remember, some with partners who I've never met, and others sitting with their children but with no man.

As Jade and her fiancé begin to exchange their vows, I can barely hear because there are so many children in the church all calling out, whining and crying. One yells when her mom slaps her and refuses to stop until she's given candy.

To my side I hear Dad whisper, "It's disgusting. Don't they know how to behave?"

I shoot him a look, hoping that he'll be quiet. My face is red. I love my mom and dad, and my older sister, Jacky, but it's not always easy living in this family. I stand here feeling embarrassed, hoping that no one heard him, but I understand what he means, because I can't believe that my cousins, aunts and uncles don't seem to know how to behave either...they're very different from Mom and Dad. I feel ashamed as I think it, because I don't want to sound snobby like my parents can sometimes sound when they talk about the rest of the family. But I can't help knowing just what they mean, as the yelling of children and hissing of their parents drowns out, "I now pronounce you man and wife."

I'm glad when the bride and groom walk back down the aisle beaming at everyone and it's finally over. We file out of the church and make our way outside, where the wind is blowing so hard that I have to hold my hat on. Stupid thing, it's flattening my hair and I know I look silly, but Mom insisted that I wear it. She said that it was "only right and proper" that her daughters should do things the "correct" way, so despite our protests she was adamant that we should wear a hat to the wedding. I long for it to all be over; then I can change back into my jeans and feel more comfortable.

We're being ushered into a group so that photos can be taken, and I stand close to Jacky. Dad tells us to stand by them, and it feels like he's trying to keep us in a little isolated nucleus, safe from the rest of the family.

It's finally over and we get into the car. I know what's going to happen.

"Did you see the state of Jade?" Mom says. "I wouldn't have had the nerve to dress in white or walk down the aisle if I were pregnant. She might at least have waited until the baby was born."

"I think the whole thing's a farce. They'll be divorced by the time the kid's a year old," Dad says.

Jacky looks at me and raises her eyes to the heavens.

"And did you see the way those children behaved in church? It was a disgrace."

"Well, what d'you expect when there are no fathers in the home?"

"Did you see Bill's oldest daughter, the one in the bright pink short skirt? She's much too old to be wearing clothes like that."

Uncle Bill is Dad's oldest brother, and Dad's ashamed of him; said he was always "bad." He has never married but has lots of kids by different women. I don't know any of them and Dad won't let us know them.

"How old is she?" Mom asks.

"Nearly thirty, I think, and she's got six kids by six different men."

He shakes his head, "Terrible...still, it's no surprise when that's the example her dad gave her."

"That's right," Mom says.

"Jade's dress was beautiful," I say, trying to stop them from assassinating the rest of the family before we get to the reception, but I should have saved my breath.

"How did she afford it," Mom said, "with her being on welfare?"

Jacky nudges me and shakes her head, warning me not to even try to stick up for them all. "Greg's coming to the reception later. Is Linda?"

Greg is Jacky's boyfriend...they're madly in love, and he's all she can talk about. I like him but Mom and Dad love him because he's planning to go to medical school. Linda is my best friend, and I'm so grateful that I can bring her to the reception be-cause I'd be really bored if she weren't here.

We pull up in front of the restaurant and she's sitting on the wall.

"Cool hat," she laughs.

"Don't," I say, trying to unpin it.

"Here, let me."

She finds the pins and suddenly my head is free. I bend over and ruffle my fingers through my hair to make it go the way I want it to.

"That's better."

"Are all these people your family?" she asks, staring around at everyone standing in groups, look-ing at each other's outfits and whispering behind their hands.

"Yep. I'm so glad you're here." I grin at her.

"Your family's worse than mine and that's saying something," she laughs. "I can't believe how many children there are. Do you know all their names?"

Two kids grab hold of me as one chases the other, ignoring their moms who shout, "Get over here, or you'll get a whooping."

"I don't know half these people," I tell her. "Both my parents come from big families, and they've all got lots of kids. Don't say anything in front of my parents about it or you'll start them off. They really disapprove of the way their families live their lives...ouch!"

A kid stomps on my toe as he tries to catch

another one who's weaving in and out of the adults' legs as we all wait to go into the restaurant.

"...And I don't blame them, really," I say, hopping on one foot with tears in my eyes.

Mom and Dad walk over to us.

"Don't mind our family," Dad says to Linda. "Glad you could come and keep Hannah company."

Linda grins at him and says, "My family's just the same; thanks for letting me come."

Finally we're allowed to go inside and Dad gets us a table near the door and as far away from the buffet as possible. He says that they'll swarm all over the food, and at least sitting over here he won't have to endure their bad table manners. I hate that he says such things, but as they all rush to the buffet and push in line, I can see that what he says is true.

We line up and virtually everything's gone by the time we get to the food. Mom's nostrils are flaring with disgust as she sees everyone walking by with their plates piled high and not caring about the people coming behind them.

We sit back down with virtually empty plates, not that I care because suddenly I'm not very hungry anymore. Everyone's talking with their mouths full, and I can see chewed up food churning around their mouths as they shout across the table. Linda's giggling and she digs me in the ribs, nodding towards Aunt Sue who's got chocolate cake on her nose as she shovels spoonfuls into her mouth. Mom and Dad don't have to hide their feelings anymore because the noise is so loud that they can say what they like without being overheard. Jacky is oblivious to it all as she stares into Greg's eyes.

Mom embarrasses me in front of Linda when she says, "I'm so proud of our girls; they're so good. Jacky's doing well at college and Hannah's working hard at her grades. They're so different from everyone in this family. I mean, look around you, it's as if none of us belongs here at all."

The speeches go on and on, and Mom and Dad stare stony-faced, as the jokes get dirtier and dirtier. When it's all over and the tables are moved back so that everyone can start dancing, Dad tells us we're going home because he can't stand anymore.

"It's only six o'clock," Linda says. "D'you think that your parents will let you go to Zak's birthday party?"

I know my face lights up. Zak is sort of my boyfriend. I'm fifteen, but my parents won't let me date yet. They tell me that I've got to concentrate on my grades so that I can go to college like Jacky, and they constantly drum into us that we are not going to turn out like the rest of the family. "I don't know. I'll ask."

Jacky's gone off with Greg, and as Linda and I sit in the back of the car, Mom says, "Well, I'm starving, shall we go for a meal?" Linda glances at me.

"Um, Mom, Dad, since we've left the wedding so

early, do you mind if I go to a party with Linda?"

Dad glances over his shoulder as he drives. "Whose party?"

Linda answers, "It's just one of the girls at school, sir; it's her birthday. Her parents will be there and it'll end by midnight."

I shoot her a look; she's just lied to my mom and dad.

"What d'you think?" he asks Mom.

"Well, if the girl's parents are going to be there it should be okay, but we'll pick you up."

"Thanks," Linda says. "We'll be waiting outside the door at the time you tell us to be ready."

"Thanks," I say, my stomach churning. I don't like lying to my parents because, although they can be stuffy, I know that they've worked very hard to give Jacky and me everything that they didn't have. I always wondered why they kept us away from the family as we grew up, and as I became a teenager they told me why.

Dad and Mom met at college, and when they told their story about how they met, their eyes misted over and they went to a place that excluded Jacky and me. They laughed when they told us the lengths they went to in order to avoid telling the other that they'd grown up in poverty with alcoholic parents and knowing how it felt to have no clothes or proper food.

"My knees were always poking through my jeans,"

Dad had said, "and I wore my brother's when he got too big for them. I didn't mind, though, I was just grateful."

He'd told me how he heard his mother crying at night when she thought that she was all alone, after his dad had beaten her and gone to the local bar. He said that it twisted his heart in pain to hear her and be unable to do anything to help. She died when he was nine years old, and he and his brothers and sisters had virtually brought themselves up while his dad went out to bars each night. He's told Jacky and me over and over how he was determined to be a good husband and father, and how much he wanted to make things different for his own family.

Mom had a hard time too, and she told us that her mother was an alcoholic, so she and her brothers and sisters had also brought themselves up while her mom was drunk on the couch. Her dad had left, and she hadn't seen him since she was ten; she was left to take care of her younger brothers and sisters.

Mom and Dad met when they were at college. He was studying engineering during the day and worked at night to pay for his education, and Mom did the same, only she studied travel and tourism. It's through her work as a travel agent that we've been to so many parts of the world, and I'm so grateful for everything they've done for us. It's not been easy, though, because both Mom and Dad's families resent the fact that they've done well for themselves in order to make a different life, and most of the family arguments stem from their jealousy. I find it hard to understand why Mom and Dad still bother with their families if they cause them so much pain, but they say that "blood is thicker than water," and they hope to be an example for all the nieces and nephews.

I know how much my parents have sacrificed for Jacky and me, especially after today when I could see for myself how different they are from their families, so I hate lying to them.

Linda looks pleased and I give her a bleak smile. I'm glad to be able to go to Zak's party—in fact, I can't wait to see him—but I wish that she hadn't lied so that I could go.

Mom and Dad drop us off at home so that we can get ready, and they head off to eat something better than the leftovers of the wedding buffet, saying that they'll pick us up at 11:30.

I'm not hungry; my stomach's a mess and my hands are trembling as I try to do my eyes. I'm mad at myself as I mess up and have to start all over again. Linda tugs at my arm and hands me a bottle of soda, saying, "Here, have one of my special sodas, it'll make you feel better."

"What's in it?"

"Vodka. I took it from my dad's cupboard. It's good and you can't smell it on your breath."

She grins at me and takes a swig from the bottle,

and not wanting to be left out I take the bottle from her hand and swallow hard. It burns my throat and my eyes open wide with surprise. Then as warmth seeps through me, I sit in a comfy chair and hand her my eye makeup so that she can do it for me.

"Cool," I say, taking another swig from the bottle as I look at my face in the mirror; it's flushed.

"You look great. C'mon, let's go."

I follow her out of the house and we walk up the road. She makes me laugh as we walk the mile to Zak's house, and by the time we get there I'm excited and feeling very woozy.

I've never been to a party before, and kids are everywhere, hanging around the outside of the house, kissing on the veranda, and there's loud music coming from inside the house. I'm really excited, and Linda tops up my soda bottle with vodka before we go inside the house. Zak sees me almost immediately and comes over to us.

"Hey, I thought you weren't going to be able to come tonight. Weren't you supposed to be going to a family wedding or something?"

"Yes, I went but it was awful so my parents left early."

"Cool, come and get yourself a drink."

I follow him to the kitchen and he pours something—I don't know what—into a glass and hands it to me. His eyes are shining at me and my stomach is churning so badly that I'm afraid my hands will tremble and I'll drop my drink. He's filled it to the top, and to avoid spilling it down my front and embarrassing myself, I take a big swig. As it flows down my throat, I gasp. It burns more than the vodka did; this makes my eyes sting and my nose prickle with its fumes.

He takes my hand. "Come and dance with me," he says.

I'm feeling so dizzy and separated from myself that I let him pull me along the hall back into the living room where everyone's dancing, and I bop about to the rhythm, giggling and laughing as he moves around me. Linda's in some boy's arms, someone from school I think, and she grins at me, nodding, making a thumbs up sign behind the boy's back.

Zak pulls me to him as the music changes, and I feel as if I'm on fire, everything inside me alive and urgent as he grinds himself into me in time to the music. I don't resist when he clamps his mouth over mine and kisses me hard. It's as if the music and all the kids disappear to somewhere beyond this moment in time, this moment in my life where I feel special and alive. He sways into me as the music changes again and then laughs, pulling away from me but still holding my hands as he moves his body in time to the music. It's so loud that I can hear the beat vibrating through my feet and up to my chest, and as the house rocks, so do I.

Linda grabs my hand, pulling me away from Zak

and she dances with me.

"Great party," she shouts above the noise, and then she struts off to dance with another group of kids.

I stagger off towards the kitchen and bump up against both walls as I zigzag along the hallway. I need to drink some water. I need to throw up—the room's going round and round and I feel awful.

There's no one in the kitchen and I steady myself at the sink, holding on as if I'm lost at sea and clinging to a piece of stray debris. I find a glass that's got lipstick on the rim, but I don't care. I just need to get some water inside of me, so I fill it and drink thirstily from the clean side.

"There you are," Zak says thickly. "I looked for you, but you'd gone."

"I was thirsty. I also need the bathroom," I slur.

"Here, let me help you," he says, grabbing my arm and leading me out of the kitchen.

I'm wobbling all over the place as he helps me up the stairs to the bathroom.

"Go on, I'll wait outside," he says.

He opens the door and I go in, staggering, falling against the wall, and I try to steady myself as I sit down. The room is going round and round and there's a loud humming in my head that has no rhythm or tune—it's just a noise, one that takes control of my head and lets me know that I've lost control of myself and my senses.

I manage to pull my panties back up and head for the door, but when I step out into the hall I feel so dizzy that I fall into Zak's arms. I'm grateful that he's there or else I'd have landed facedown on the floor.

"Hey, are you all right?" he asks, but I can't answer for I don't know if the weakness I'm feeling is due to the alcohol I've drunk or the longing I feel riding through my body as he starts to kiss me again.

He leads me to his bedroom but I don't remember getting there. I don't remember how I ended up on his bed without my panties on, beneath his posters of baseball heroes and rap artists. But I know without coherent words that, as I lie there on his bed with alcohol soaring through me and the room spinning round and round, he's just entered my body. I'm too dizzy to respond because all I can think of is that I'm going to throw up all over his bed, so as I'm gripping the bed trying to anchor myself to a stable point that won't keep spinning around the room, he pushes and pushes into me.

I don't know how it all happened. All I can really remember is that he thrust his trashcan under my nose as I leaned over the bed, throwing up harder than I can ever remember doing before. The humming in my head is as loud as ever, and as I keep my head close to the trashcan, three feelings jostle about in my mind. I can't believe that I'm throwing up in front of the boy I like. Then I can't believe that I've just had sex with him—it's my first time and I'm so drunk that I can't remember anything about it. And the last feeling is that I want to die and make it all go away.

Somewhere I'm aware that he's looking really worried as I continue to retch, and after a timeless moment that slips into nothingness, I'm aware that Linda's kneeling by his bed.

"Are you all right?" she asks, looking worried.

"Uh? What?"

"It's nearly time for your dad to pick us up," she says.

I'm jolted back into this room, Zak's bedroom—oh my God, what have I done? I start to cry. My dad'll kill me if he sees me drunk, and then it dawns on me—my dad would kill me if he knew that tonight I lost my virginity through "casual sex" and couldn't even remember it.

Zak and Linda pull me off the bed, and I sway as they lead me down the stairs and into the kitchen, where they force me to drink loads of water. Tears are rolling down my face as I throw up again all over the kitchen floor. I'm so ashamed of myself and so embarrassed because, although everything is still spinning around the room, I catch sight of the disgust on Zak's face.

Linda's hissing in my face, "Come on, Hannah, we've got to get outside because your dad will be here in a minute."

She pulls me up and I stand there swaying, feeling terrible, but that's nothing compared to how I feel when I turn around and see my dad in the doorway.

"What the..." he says.

I know that in one second he has scanned the room, seen me dishevelled, wobbly and a pool of vomit on the floor, and he knows exactly what's been going on.

"Where are your friend's parents?" he demands.

Zak says, "They're not here; they've gone away for the weekend."

"Who are you?" Dad asks rudely.

"I'm Zak; it's my party."

Dad glares at Linda. "You told me that the party was to celebrate a girl friend's birthday and that her parents would be here."

Linda looks down at the floor and mutters, "Sorry."

"We're leaving, right now," he says, glaring at Zak and completely ignoring me.

Linda helps me through the crowd of kids who all stop dancing to watch my humiliation as my dad marches through the house and I stagger behind him.

He opens the car door and barks, "Get in," and we sit in silence as he drives.

"I'm really disappointed in you, Linda. I hate

being lied to. If that's the kind of girl you are, I don't want my daughter to associate with you. I don't want you coming around."

"Dad!" I cry.

"I'm so sorry," Linda begs.

"No! Enough! Every behavior has a consequence, and if neither of you can be trusted, then you have to suffer the consequences. You're not welcome around my house, Linda, and you, my girl, are grounded."

I'm crying, but Linda looks angry and sullen, and as Dad pulls up outside her house, she gets out of the car and says loudly, "I'll see you at school, Hannah," and then she slams the door.

Dad drives off.

"You are to stay away from her, do you hear me? I don't want you being with someone like that, not now, not ever. Look at the state of you, you're drunk and you look like a slut dressed like that. You look just like your cousins. Haven't I brought you up to be better than that? Haven't I?"

"I'm sorry, Dad," I cry.

"Sorry's not good enough. Did *you* know that the party was not at your girl friend's house?"

I nod miserably; I don't want to lie to him further.

"So you lied to me, too. I'm really disappointed in you, Hannah. Haven't Mom and I done everything we could to give you a good life so that you don't end up like your cousins and all that mess? Is that what you want—to end up like them?"

"No," I howl.

"Well, you could have fooled me. Can't you see what drinking alcohol does to people, to families? Surely Mom and I have told you enough times what it did to our parents and how we suffered through it as children. Can't you learn from our experiences? Where did you get it from, anyway?"

He looks over his shoulder at me and his face holds a mixture of anger and pain.

"Linda gave me some and then I had some more at Zak's house," I say miserably.

"Well, I don't want you to go anywhere near her anymore, do you hear me? And I'll be going round to see Zak's parents as soon as they're back."

I'm crying hard now, thinking of the trouble my dad will cause Zak.

"Please don't, Dad, please," I plead.

His face is set, his jaw grim.

"He'll hate me and tell everyone at school, and then they'll hate me, too. It's not his fault. Please don't tell his parents."

I can tell that he's really angry because he drives fast and erratically, swerving around corners. And although I've got my seat belt on, I grab the handle above the door. My stomach's churning really badly and, before I can cry out to ask him to stop, I vomit all down my favorite top. He shrieks to a stop on our driveway.

"Get out," he shouts, his face screwed up. "Look what you've done to my car...you'll clean that up, right now."

I'm crying all over again as he tells me to stay outside. I feel so ill and utterly humiliated standing beneath the outside light with moths zooming around my head. Mom comes out with a bucket of soapy water and her tongue.

"How could you, Hannah? We trusted you. How could you lie and then get yourself in such a state? You're no better than your cousins; and after all we've done for you to help you turn out differently from them. Clean your dad's car up and don't come back in until it's spotless. Oh, and by the way, you're grounded for a month."

She marches back inside the house and leaves me on my knees scrubbing Dad's upholstery. It's gross but not as bad as it could be, because I'd already lost most of the contents of my stomach earlier. I'm relieved because I can't stand mopping up vomit; it makes me heave even more—the smell, and the bits of carrot that always seem to be there even if you haven't eaten them.

When I'm done I slip into the house and head for the stairs, hoping that Mom and Dad won't hear me, but it's no good. They appear from nowhere and I feel as if they've been lying in wait, ready to pounce on me to remind me of what a disappointment I've been to them.

# Chapter Two

I wake up the next morning with incredible pain in my head—it's pounding really badly—and I feel so sick. I feel as if I could drink a swimming pool and even then my thirst wouldn't be quenched. If this is what drinking alcohol does to you, then you can keep it, it's not worth the agony the next day. Okay, it made me laugh to start with and I felt as if I could do anything, but then it all changed without any warning. That's when the room started spinning and I knew that no matter what I did to try and stop it, I was going to throw up. The nausea had no respect for where I was or whom I was with, it was determined to project its mess and my humiliation for all to see...and they saw. I'll never live it down at school, and I doubt if Zak will ever speak to me again.

As his name pops into my mind, my face reddens

with shame. I can't believe what I did, and I know that I would never have done it if I hadn't been drunk. He was only "sort of" my boyfriend, I wasn't even really going out with him. I feel so sick that I can't tell if it's due to my hangover or to being so ashamed of myself.

I get up and go to the bathroom and peer into the mirror. My eyes look raw and are puffy from all the crying I've done. As I come out, Jacky's waiting to go into the bathroom and I avoid her gaze.

"Oops," she says kindly, "I hear you're in a bit of trouble." There's no malice in her voice; in fact, she sounds gentle. I start to cry and she follows me into my room.

"What happened?"

I tell her everything. "Linda lied to Mom and Dad about where the party was and I didn't say anything, but worse was that she gave me vodka and I drank it. It's not her fault, I mean, I could have said 'No' but I didn't want to. It seemed fun at first, but then I was so drunk that I couldn't stand up, and worse, I vomited everywhere."

She smiles at me; I love that she's so kind to me. We used to argue when we were both younger.

"I remember my first time, too; it was awful. Don't beat yourself up about it, babe, Mom and Dad will get over it. I think they were more upset about you lying to them, well, and vomiting in Dad's car." Her face slips into a slight grin. "I don't think they're very keen about your friend either. It might be a good idea not to mention her around here for a while."

I feel awful. "Dad was so rude to her last night, and to my friend Zak. I know I embarrassed Dad, but he embarrassed me, too."

"Don't be too hard on him, Hannah. You know Mom and Dad want something different for us after having a real hard time as kids themselves. He only wants what's best for us."

"I know, but he made me feel like dirt, and I was already feeling ashamed of myself without him making it worse."

"Try and understand where they're coming from. You saw what Mom and Dad's families are like; they've both fought to make a good life for themselves and us, and I think they're terrified that they'll end up back where they started from. It makes them overreact at times."

I sit quietly staring at the floor and she pats my hand. She sounds so old and wise.

"Listen, you aren't the first kid to get drunk and you won't be the last. Drinking alcohol isn't good for you, we all know that, and it can leave you in situations that can hurt you or even kill you." She grins at me. "Know what my girl friend told me?"

I shake my head.

She's still grinning at me. "There are two rules about drinking alcohol because it can be so dangerous. The first is a rule for everyone, and that is to sleep on your stomach, so that you don't vomit in your sleep and suffocate yourself, and the second rule is for us girls...keep your panties on."

My face is brilliant red, and I pray she doesn't notice.

"It's easy to do something that you wouldn't normally do if you were sober. Remember those two rules, Hannah, and you'll be okay."

I find my voice. "Don't worry, I'm never getting drunk again."

She goes off to the bathroom and I'm left with my flushed face, and my guilt and shame.

I put my robe on and venture downstairs, dreading meeting Mom and Dad, but I have to face them sometime so I'd better get it over with. Dad's sitting at the kitchen table reading his paper, and Mom's making pancakes. Neither looks up when I enter the room. Their indifference hurts but I guess I deserve it, so I plunge into an apology.

"I'm so sorry I lied to you, I didn't mean to. I just didn't want to show Linda up...I didn't know she was going to lie...I don't know why she did. I just didn't know what to do, so I did nothing. I'm sorry. And I'm sorry for throwing up in your car, Dad."

"I'm really disappointed in you, Hannah. I thought you knew better. How can we trust you again if you're going to behave like that?"

"I promise you, I'll never do it again."

"Well, that may be so, but you're still grounded for a month and we don't want you to have anything to do with Linda."

"But she's my friend, we're in the same classes at school. I can't ignore her."

"I thought you had better judgment than to choose that type of friend," Dad says, and I feel really angry with him. Linda may have made a mistake by lying, and I don't know why she did it—perhaps she has the type of parents that you have to defend yourself against, I don't know—but she's my friend, and a good one.

"You don't know her," I dare to say. "She's good and kind."

Mom shoots me a look that warns me to be quiet.

"She lied and put my daughter at risk," Dad says, as if daring me to challenge him, but I have to, for she *is* my friend.

"I don't know why she lied, Dad, I don't understand it, but I know that she's a good person, and it's not her fault that I got drunk. I should have said 'No,' that's what I should have done, but I didn't. It's me you should blame, not her."

"If she hadn't given you the alcohol, you wouldn't have gotten drunk and embarrassed yourself," and then his face contorts, "and you wouldn't have hurt me and your mother."

Jacky walks into the kitchen and pours herself a cup of coffee.

"Dad, Hannah will face all kinds of people offering her things—alcohol, marijuana, and recreational drugs, and even the hard stuff like heroin...it's all out there, it's everywhere. You can't blame other people. Hannah has to have the strength to say 'No,' and if she doesn't, then she has to take responsibility for the choices she makes and the consequences of those choices."

Mom smiles at Jacky and I love her for smoothing everything down, because Dad becomes quieter and goes back to his paper.

"D'you want pancakes and syrup, Hannah?" Mom asks, and she raises an eyebrow as I rush out of the room and head for the bathroom, gagging.

Most of the day passes with me confined to my bedroom, not only because I'm grounded, but because I feel so bad that all I want to do is lie on my bed and drink gallons of water. There's school tomorrow and I can't wait to see Linda, partly to talk about the party but also to apologize for my dad's attitude towards her. I also want to ask her why she lied when she didn't have to.

I drift in and out of sleep, and the hours seem to glide by in a dehydrated haze where I long to saturate myself in water and sleep for a week until my body recovers from the poisons I willingly put into it.

I go to the bathroom for yet another glass of water, and I can't believe that the whole day's gone by. I go downstairs and Mom's cooking dinner...I manage to stop myself from gagging.

"Where's Dad?" I ask.

She seems flustered. "Out, just out."

She mashes the potatoes and tells me to put the silverware out on the table.

My head hurts so badly and my stomach is raw; I don't want anything to eat, but I do as she says.

She has everything ready but Dad's still not home. The smell of chicken turns my stomach and I rush back upstairs, just barely making it to the bathroom before I throw up again. As I wash my face, I hear the slam of the door and my dad's raised voice.

"Well, I can't believe it. What awful people...of course they stuck up for their son, I think the kid's name is Zak..."

My stomach does a double flip. No, don't tell me he actually went over to their house. I feel even more sick, though there's nothing in my stomach. How can I face Zak at school tomorrow?

"They were awful and took an attitude with me. They said it wasn't their fault that my daughter was drunk. They wouldn't take any responsibility at all. They shouldn't be keeping liquor in the house when they're not there. What kind of people are they? I told them that they ought to know their child better and take more of an interest in him, then they'd know whether they could trust him to be left alone or not."

Mom falters and I strain to hear her from the top of the stairs.

"What did they say to that?" she asks.

I'm trembling because it gets worse.

"Well, I can't believe how rude they were. They told me that I should leave before they called the police."

He makes this noise with his mouth that tells me he's in one of his moods, the one where he's right and the rest of the human race is wrong.

"So I told them to go ahead and call them...I'd be glad to report them for allowing their home to be used for underage drinking."

He sounds so pompous. I know that tone of voice. It's the one he's been using since we got Jade's wedding invitation in the mail...like he's better than anyone else.

"You didn't?" Mom says.

"Of course I did."

Dad sounds surprised that she should ask, and he rounds on her.

"Surely you feel the same? Parents should know what their children are up to and not put themselves first by going away overnight."

"Yes, but..." she doesn't finish.

I feel faint, imagining the repercussions going on in Zak's house. If my dad said those things to Zak's parents, they'll be mad and will take it out on him. Okay, so he shouldn't have had a party without their permission, but my dad's made it ten times worse for him. He seems determined to distance himself from people who live by what he calls "substandards" and who he believes are poor parents. I know he had a hard time as a kid, but does he need to be so pompous and self-righteous all the time?

I creep back into my bedroom and sit on the bed with the door open. I honestly don't know how I'm going to face Zak at school now; he'll hate me, and who can blame him. Nor do I know how I'm going to go downstairs and face Dad without exploding, for I'm so mad at him. Isn't it enough punishment that I've been grounded for a month? Why did he have to go and tell Zak's parents? It's not his business if their son had a party while they were away. What makes my dad so determined to dish out punishment to kids that aren't even his?

I can hear Jacky come through the door downstairs. "What's up?" she says, instantly aware that something's wrong by the tone of Dad's voice.

"Your mother doesn't agree that I did the right thing by going over to that boy's parents, and telling them their son was encouraging underage drinking."

"I didn't say that," Mom says, and I can imagine her shaking her head, trying to distance herself from the things he's saying.

"Well, you didn't exactly back me up," he accuses.

Mom sounds upset. "I just think it might have been better not to be so angry, because it's more likely to make them stick up for their son, even if he did wrong."

I hear Dad slam the kitchen door and I know he's gone outside to water his plants, and that means he's mad.

I venture down the stairs, relieved beyond belief that Jacky's home.

"Don't worry, Mom, he'll get over it," she says.

I stand in the doorway feeling as if I've brought damnation upon my family just because I got drunk and threw up everywhere. It feels crazy. I know I shouldn't have, and I was wrong to lie, but I didn't kill anyone, and Jacky said that most kids do it once and vow never to do it again. She makes it sound like an initiation rite into adulthood, like playing at being adult, like trying on a new and bigger shoe to see if it fits; it's like playing at being grown up...thinking you can handle it but learning that you can't.

I suddenly feel tearful because I know that I'm not a child but I'm not an adult either, so what am I? I don't really know, and it's a horrible feeling. I've upset my mom and dad, and Dad's gone off in a temper because now he's angry with Mom, and Mom's upset because she was trying to be reasonable but ended up being misunderstood. All this because of me.

I don't sleep very well, and as I get dressed

there's a gnawing fear in my stomach thinking about how school's going to be today. I can't wait to see Linda, to apologize for my dad's rudeness. Okay, she shouldn't have lied to him, and I still can't work out why she did, but she didn't deserve him being so rude to her.

I eat a piece of toast that tastes like cardboard and set off.

"Don't forget, you're grounded," Mom calls out as I go to slam the door. As if I could forget!

I can't remember walking to school because my mind is full of everything that's happened this weekend. A feeling of dread mounts inside me as I go through the school gates and walk towards the entrance.

I swallow hard as I begin to climb the stone steps because Zak and his friends are lolling around, leaning on the railings, whispering to each other. There's nowhere else to go but up the steps towards the entrance, and I wonder what's going to happen. I don't have long to wait, for Zak's friend shouts out to me.

"Did you tell Daddy everything?"

My face is burning. I knew this would happen. Zak's told all his friends what my Dad did. I open my mouth to speak, to tell them that I'm as angry as they are for what he did, but then everything changes.

Zak stops me and grabs my arm, hissing into my

face. "So it's all my fault, is it? D'you know what my parents did to me because of your father and his mouth? Look," he spits.

He has a black eye, and the sight of it makes me sick. I'm angry at my pompous, self-righteous father.

I shake my head not knowing how to answer.

"And d'you know what? They let me know just how much they think of me," he says sarcastically. "Well, it's payback time...I'm going to let everyone know what I think of you, so that you'll know how I feel," and as he finishes speaking he reaches into his pocket.

I'm completely mortified as he pulls out my pink, lacy panties. I can feel the color drain from my face and my head begins to spin. I've been in such denial about what happened at the party, focusing only on drinking too much and embarrassing myself by vomiting everywhere, that I haven't dared allow myself to think about what I did with Zak, or that I left my panties in his room. Until now I haven't even given them another thought.

Panic flows through me as he holds my panties up like a flag, a trophy for everyone to see. My humiliation is complete, but he doesn't stop there. He starts shouting and waving them at the kids coming into school.

"Hey, everyone, what d'you think? Does Hannah look good in pink?"

I watch in horror as he waves my panties in front of all the kids, who snicker and point at me as they go into school.

My face is raw with shame. I'd conveniently forgotten that somehow my panties had been removed at the party...I really don't know if I took them off or if he edged them down over my hips and knees while I was so drunk that I didn't have a clue what was going on. How it happened doesn't matters, though, all that matters now is that my humiliation is flapping around in the wind as he waves my panties with the same pride that a patriot would wave a state flag.

I try to snatch them from him but he's taller than me and waves them high above my head, then throws them to his friends, and I'm caught in a bizarre and humiliating game of "catch."

I can't go inside and get a teacher to help me because then they'll know of my shame, and I don't know what to do to make him stop or to make him give them back.

"What would Daddy say if I mailed them to him?" Zak sneers, and I feel as if my spine has just turned to ice.

I turn and run into school, desperate to get away from him and his friends. I can't go to class because I'm crying so hard, so I go to the bathroom, run some water, and splash my face with my trembling hands.

The bathroom door bursts open and Linda comes over to me.

"I can't believe it," she says. "All the kids are talking about it. Don't you worry, I'll get them back for you."

"He says he's going to mail them to my Dad. I have to get them back; I just have to."

She hands me a paper towel, and with grim determination on her face she says, "Trust me, Hannah, I'll get them back for you. Now, come on, let's get to class before we have to start explaining all this to the principal."

She drags me out of the bathroom and pushes me through the door into class. I can hear kids whispering and snickering at the back of the room.

"Ignore them," Linda hisses.

Our teacher raises his voice and holds out his hand to silence everyone.

"Pay attention!" he shouts. "Today we have a guest speaker, Miss Tina, who works with teenagers."

He doesn't leave the room but sits at his table marking some papers, while the lady stands in front of us and smiles.

"Hi, my name is Miss Tina and I work at a place called Beach Haven. It's a place where we help young people to understand themselves and to cope with the problems they face during adolescence. Being a teenager can be tough."

Tell me about it...

"Today we're going to look at coping with peer pressure and drinking alcohol."

Kids murmur behind me and Linda looks at me with guilt on her face.

The teacher looks up and gives us one of his stares, and everyone goes quiet.

"What is peer pressure?" Miss Tina asks.

"What it says," some smart-mouthed kid says. "Pressure put on you by your peers."

The teacher looks over his glasses, but Miss Tina seems unfazed.

"And what is the purpose of putting pressure on your peers?"

No one answers. The teacher lays his pen down and looks at us.

Miss Tina doesn't point to anyone to answer, but says, "The purpose of peer pressure is to force others to *conform* to what the majority are doing."

Linda glances at me and I smile weakly at her. I guess she feels bad, but so do I.

"Why is it so important to conform to your peers?" she asks.

"So that you'll be accepted by the gang," a kid shouts out.

"So that you'll be liked, or be popular."

"To belong."

"So that people won't call you a dork."

Miss Tina smiles at us. "Y'know, being a teenager is tough. It's a time when you're no longer a child but you're not quite an adult. It's a time of uncertainty, a time when you wear many hats to see what fits and who you're going to be."

"Hats?" a kid shouts out.

"Yes, that means to try out different ways of being to see what feels the most comfortable to you. It's a time of self-discovery...are you quiet or loud, studious or outgoing? Are you good with people or do you feel more comfortable being alone with computers or books? Do you have burning ambitions, or are you the sort of person who's happy with what turns up?"

I try to listen to her, but my thoughts are racing, thinking about how I can get my panties back so that Zak can't mail them to my dad. I have an overwhelming urge to cry.

"Being a teenager is a time when you try out different roles to see who the real you is, and it's also a time when you begin to break away from your parents and how they see you, and that may be very different from the way you see yourself."

I don't want to explore the way I see myself right now as I feel so bad; I'm having trouble concentrating on what she's saying...all I can think of is Zak and what he's planning to do.

"So much uncertainty inside forces teenagers to band together with other kids to help them feel... um...safe and secure...it's normal. Sometimes that can be helpful but other times it can be harmful. Who can suggest why?" she asks.

"Well, if you band together with kids who're doing things that their parents approve of...well...you'll stay out of trouble, but if you band together with kids who do stuff that your parents disapprove of, then you could get into trouble...depending on what it was..."

"That's a good answer," Miss Tina says, "and it's exactly right. When can peer pressure be helpful?"

"When your friends make you join their church or team and nag you to keep going, even if you don't want to."

"When your friends force you to keep your grades up even when you can't be bothered."

"Yes, definitely," she says, smiling at us. My stomach starts to churn because I know what she's going to ask next.

"When can banding together be harmful?"

Everyone's silent.

"C'mon, think about it. When is peer pressure harmful?"

Linda looks at me with regret on her face, and she speaks out.

"When you put pressure on someone to do something that they wouldn't normally do."

"Like what?" Miss Tina presses.

Linda glances at me again and I look down.

"Drink alcohol," she says.

Miss Tina nods. "Yes, there is a lot of peer pressure to drink alcohol, and it's a tough one because it's legal and lots of parents do it, so where do you draw the line? When does it shift from becoming okay and acceptable to becoming harmful?"

"When you do things that you wouldn't normally do if you were sober," the teacher says, unable to stop himself from joining in.

Miss Tina smiles at him, and says, "Yes, like what?"

We all stare at him, wondering what he does when he's drunk that he wishes he hadn't done. He shrugs and goes quiet.

"What kind of things would you do when you're drunk that you wouldn't do when you're sober?" she asks us.

My stomach churns and my head is spinning. I'm only vaguely aware of kids calling out, although I do hear the words, "unprotected sex" and "kicking off."

My thoughts drift and Miss Tina's voice fades as images of me throwing up in front of everyone at Zak's party and again in my dad's car—and worst of all, losing my panties—flood my mind.

I try and force my thoughts to stay on what Miss Tina's saying about peer pressure, but they drift again. I felt peer pressure on the night of the party...I didn't want Linda to think I was a dork, and I wanted Zak to want me. I drank, even though I knew my dad wouldn't approve, because I wanted to be accepted by Linda and all the kids at the party, especially Zak.

I know that if I'd been sober I wouldn't have had sex with Zak...he wasn't even a proper boyfriend... yeah, I liked him and he seemed to like me, but he'd never said that we were going together.

My face is burning.

I don't blame Linda because I know my actions were my responsibility, and weren't her fault...I should've been strong enough to say "no," and even if she was mad at me, I should've stood up for myself. I could still have gone to the party and had a good time; I didn't need to get wrecked by drinking so much alcohol.

I can't hear Miss Tina anymore as I drift away, lost in my own self-recriminations, and the image of my pink, lacy panties being waved in the wind by Zak, like a trophy telling everyone that he's had me, fills my mind.

# Chapter Three

I don't know how I get through the day. At each break Zak and his friends taunt me and wave my panties at me in front of crowds of kids, who all laugh. Linda yells insults at him when the teachers aren't looking, but it doesn't do any good.

At the end of school I have to go straight home because I'm grounded. I feel stupid being grounded at my age—it makes me feel like a little kid—but I go along with it because I don't want to upset my mom and dad...besides, if I do as they ask, they're more likely to relent and lift my curfew. They constantly tell me that "Every behavior has a consequence," so if I show them good behavior they might give me a good consequence and let me go out, or at least stay late at school.

I want to join the running club as I've always been able to run fast; and then there's the trampoline club, but I don't suppose there'll be any spare spaces by the time my grounding is lifted.

I walk home alone, miserably. Linda's at the gym practicing for the cheerleader try-outs. I wanted to but I can't now...it doesn't seem fair somehow.

Mom's already home, and if she notices my miserable face, she doesn't say anything about it. She just says, "Thank you," and I assume she says it because I did as I was told. I go upstairs to my room and turn on my computer. Mom and Dad bought it for me last Christmas and said that it cost a fortune, and that I should be very grateful because they never had parents who would give them anything. I start to write an email to Linda telling her how bored I am. I do my homework and then I flick my TV on, but there's nothing to watch...or rather, I can't concentrate.

I hear Jacky and Dad come home, and after a while I venture downstairs. Jacky turns around when she sees me.

"Hi, Hannah, how was your day?"

I love my sister so much, but it hasn't always been this way. I remember when I hated her; she always seemed so much older than me. I was sent to bed loads earlier than she was, and it made me feel left out of the family. I could hear them downstairs having fun while I was sent to bed because of my age. I don't really know when things started to change between us, maybe it was when she had her first boyfriend. Suddenly she didn't want anyone to see her being mean to her younger sister, certainly not the boy she wanted to impress. It was good because it meant that she was nice to be around, and then as we got used to our new relationship she was more than nice to be around, she was my friend and someone who helped bridge the gap between me and my parents.

Dad takes one look at me and goes outside to water his plants. Mom gets busy at the sink. Jacky has an expression on her face that I've seen many times before—it's one of anxiety mingled with strength. She's determined to make things right in this family...to be the mediator.

"So, Hannah," she says again, "how was your day?"

I wish I could tell her how awful it's been, about Zak threatening me and shaming me in front of all the kids at school. But of course, I can't, so I say, "Fine."

Mom dries her hands and asks how Jacky's day was, and as they break the awkward silence, I put the silverware out on the table, trying to be useful.

When Dad comes in from the yard, Mom puts dishes on the table and the atmosphere is so heavy with silence that tears spring into my eyes. Jacky tells me to sit at the table and she rubs my back and winks at me as I pass her.

I don't think I can eat for my stomach is sick with anxiety...I can't stand this. Dad's silence is worse than his anger.

Jacky works hard to get everyone to talk, and she deliberately asks me questions.

"So, Hannah, how was school?"

I focus on her and try to ignore the fact that Dad is ignoring me. "It was good," I lie. "We had a lady come to speak to us today; she was nice. Her name was Miss Tina."

"What does she teach?" she asks.

"Oh, she's not a teacher; she works somewhere helping kids, I think."

"What did she talk about?" Jacky says, desperate to keep the conversation going, as Dad fills his mouth with food.

"She talked about peer pressure and drinking too much alcohol," I say steadily.

Dad all but chokes. "Well, it's a shame that she didn't teach you on Friday, isn't it?"

"Dad!" Jacky says.

He sounds like he hates me and it hurts so badly. I look around the table. Mom's focusing on the peas on her plate, Jacky sighs, and Dad glares at me. This is awful; the atmosphere is unbearable and I'll do anything to make it better. My voice breaks and a tear rolls down my face.

"I'm sorry, Dad, I didn't mean to upset you," I say, even though a small voice inside my head says,

"Hannah, you didn't kill anyone...maybe this isn't about you," but I silence it.

"I wish that Miss Tina had come to the school on Friday, too, because if she had, I'd have been more aware of peer pressure. And I think I'd have stuck up for myself more and not cared about what my school friends thought of me. I think I'd have been able to say 'No' to drinking alcohol, too, if we'd had that class on Friday. But we didn't, and I made a mistake. I don't know what else to say..." I croak.

I don't dare think about what else I could have said "No" to if Miss Tina had taught us on Friday instead of Monday.

The tears fall down my face as I think about what I did with Zak and how hateful he's been to me today. My feelings are torn between the pain I feel at the look of disappointment on my dad's face and the feeling of anger I feel towards him. For if he hadn't gone over to Zak's house and caused so much trouble, then Zak wouldn't be threatening me now or shaming me in front of the whole school. I sob even harder at the injustice of it all, and my parents seem to interpret my crying as remorse.

Mom says, "It's all right, Hannah, we all make mistakes, Don't cry, it'll be okay." She gets up and puts her arms around me, arms that a minute ago had no room for me.

Dad coughs awkwardly, and pushes his plate

away. "Well, you've obviously thought about it," he says.

I can't help it, but I keep crying. Why are they making such a big deal about it? I feel bad and I've said "I'm sorry" over and over. I'm not crying because of the remorse I feel at having hurt them. I'm crying because they don't understand me, and because Jacky and I have to make things right for them after they've had such a terrible childhood. And in doing so I feel like I've given up my own.

I have no idea what Jacky feels, whether she feels the same as I do, but once again she rescues me.

"Hey, c'mon Hannah, I promised to show you that website we were talking about," and she pulls me out of my chair. We go into my room, and she sits back on the bed and lets out a long sigh.

"Y'know, sometimes it's hard being in this family. I know that Mom and Dad had a hard time as kids, but they sure can overreact at times." Her eyes twinkle at me. "If they knew about the things I got into at your age, they'd freak."

A giggle seeps out of me even though my face is saturated with the tears that refuse to stop falling.

"What things?"

"Oh, I couldn't possibly say," she says, playing with me. "I wouldn't want to give you ideas."

"Go on."

"No." She shakes her head, and I know she's trying to throw me a lifeline, but at the same time she doesn't want to "give me ideas" or the message that it's okay to break our parents' rules.

She hands me a tissue. "C'mon now, stop crying. It really isn't the end of the world. Stop now."

I find it really hard to stop, as I'm not crying about getting drunk or vomiting in Dad's car. I'm crying because it's all so unfair, and because I'm terrified that Zak will mail my panties to Dad to pay me back for what Dad did, and what his parents did to him. I can't tell Jacky any of it, though, and as I cry, I think she sees me as being dramatic. I feel so alone in this family, even though I love my sister, and I know she's there for me.

She goes downstairs, and I blow my nose hard and lie back on my bed. I can hear her trying to get Dad to ease up on me.

My head hurts really badly as I try to make sense of why Dad's so mad at me, yet I find it hard. Yes, I did wrong, but what I did was nothing compared to some of the kids at school. I've always tried to be good so that Mom and Dad will be pleased with me. Some of the kids at school tease me about it, and I brush them off, even though it hurts sometimes. Why then, when I try so hard to please them and I make a mistake, are they so down on me? It all feels weird somehow.

I don't want to face Mom and Dad again tonight so I get into bed and shut my door. I can't sleep, though, and two hours later Jacky brings me a hot chocolate. She sits on my bed.

"Are you okay?" she asks.

I nod miserably.

"Try not to worry. Dad will come around in his own time," she says.

"Why's he like this?" I ask. "I know I did wrong, but he acts like I murdered someone. Some of the kids at school do things that are far worse than drinking too much and throwing up. Why's he so mad at me?"

She sighs as if it's too hard to fathom. "I think he's so afraid that you and I will turn out like his family. You saw how he behaved at Jade's wedding. I think he overreacts because he's scared, and being hard on us is his way of trying to control us so that we won't turn out like his family."

"It's not fair," is all I can think of to say as I sip the hot chocolate.

"I know, but c'mon, he means well, so don't be too hard on him. He wants what's best for us..."

She places a small kiss on my forehead, and says, "It'll all be better in the morning, you'll see," before closing my door.

I lie in the dark. I can't believe that it will be better in the morning, because I'm terrified that Zak will have mailed my panties to my dad. How will that make anything better? It'll make things ten times worse...

I toss and turn all night, and as the dawn spreads shadows across my room, I know what I have to do. I get up and go downstairs. I will wait for the mailman and intercept any packages that are addressed to Dad.

I sit curled up in a chair, shivering, but watching through the curtains, with a book on my lap in case Mom or Dad finds me up so early. I'll tell them that I've got extra homework to do and I wanted to get it done. That should please them. I realize that I'm lying again. How is it that one lie leads to another and then another? Sometimes life is just too hard to work out.

I hear Mom and Dad get up and shower, and I peep out from behind the curtains, keeping watch for the mailman.

"What're you doing up so early?" Dad demands as he comes downstairs and finds me sitting in the living room.

I snap open my book and tell him that I've got some reading to get done for school. He says, "Oh," and goes into the kitchen to fix some breakfast.

Both Jacky and Mom ask me what I'm doing up so early, but they're too busy getting ready to really listen to my excuse.

They tell me to go and shower or I'll be late for school, but I can't leave my spot by the window. Our mailman is never late. Mom says you can set your watch by him, and so I know that he's about to come down the road any minute. There's no way I can take a shower now. I stall for time and tell them that I've got to finish my chapter, and that I'm almost done.

Suddenly I see him, and he walks up our drive with mail in his hands. I feel sick.

I rush towards the door and open it as quietly as I can and step outside.

"Hi," I say. "Can I take that?"

He smiles at me, and says, "Fine. Have a nice day."

Quickly I sift through the mail. There's some junk and a couple of letters that look like bills, but no package. I feel a huge sense of relief, but it's short-lived because it means that I'm going to have to sit here each morning to intercept the mail until my panties arrive.

I put the mail on the table in the hall and then I call out that I'm going upstairs to take a shower, or else I'll be late for school.

The hot water flows over me, and I wish I could climb back into bed because I'm so tired.

Mom shouts at me to hurry, but I take as long as I can because I want to be late. I don't want to face Zak, who I know will be waiting for me on the school steps, waving my pink, lacy panties in my face so that I can feel my shame all over again.

She nags me to hurry and her irritation is easier to bear than the thought of Zak's humiliation of me, so I tune her out and take my time.

As she pulls up outside the school, she's really mad at me and says, "Don't forget that you're grounded...that means no staying late after school. You're to come straight home. And Hannah, please do as your father asks and stay away from Linda."

I say, "Yes," but I know I can't do that. Linda's my friend and I don't care if Dad doesn't like her; I do. I can't ignore her, nor will I hurt her by ignoring her. I don't say anything, though, as it'll only cause another argument. Mom drives off without waving at me. My heart's heavy as I walk up the school steps and into the building, but thankfully everyone's already in class.

I slip into my class. Linda is already at her desk and I sit next to her.

"Are you okay?" she asks.

I nod. "Just tired," I whisper. "I had to sit up and wait to see if Zak mailed my...you know, to my dad."

"Did he?" she whispers.

"No."

"Don't you worry, I'll sort this mess out today, okay?"

I wish, but I don't get to say anything as the teacher slams a book down on my desk and demands that I "get quiet," and so I do.

I try to stay focused, but it's hard, and several times the teacher jolts me from my thoughts, threatening me with detention. I try to be alert, but I can't help it; all I can think of is what Zak's going to do and how my dad will react.

Linda nudges me several times as the teacher prowls around the class searching for students who aren't paying attention, and I'm grateful. But in our last class before lunch, she's not quick enough and I'm too distracted by my thoughts.

The teacher gives me a detention for not paying attention, and I'm even more humiliated by telling him in front of all the kids, who snicker, that I can't stay after school because I'm grounded. He doesn't seem to care, not about me being grounded or about humiliating me in front of the class.

"Then you'll have to do it at lunch time," he says, as if he's won a battle.

I feel so miserable. I wish it was a week ago when all that worried me was what to wear to my cousin's wedding. I can't believe how much things can change in just a few days.

Linda tells me she'll see me later, as I go off to the detention room and she goes off to the cafeteria for lunch.

The detention teacher is as fed up as I am at having to give up his lunch break to supervise the four of us that have been given detention. He lets us know that, if it weren't for us, he could put his feet up for an hour and take a break from "you kids." I wish he would take a break; then he'd give *us* a break. It's bad enough having to sit here in silence without him picking on us.

Sitting there staring at the wall is really hard for me, because all I have in my head is images of my dad going to pick up the mail and having his disappointment in me confirmed yet again. Try as I might to think of other things, the postman keeps popping back into my head..."Nice day, sir, got your mail here. This one feels soft; it looks like someone's sent you a gift, how nice—is it your birthday...?"

I shiver as the thoughts play out in my mind. How could I have gotten myself into this mess? And even as I think it, I know the answer...alcohol.

It has to be the longest hour I've ever lived through, but finally it's over, and I'm told to hurry up to my next class. It's Tuesday, and Linda and I are in different classes, so I don't see her until break. She's waiting for me to come out of the classroom, and she's wearing a grin on her face. She slips her arm through mine and hurries me down the hall into the bathroom.

"Guess what?" she states triumphantly, and she opens her schoolbag. There are my pink panties.

"How? How'd you do it?"

She grins. "My brother's got lots of friends, more friends than Zak's got; bigger too."

I throw my arms around her, and we jump up and down on the spot.

"What happened?" I ask, when I calm down.

She looks a bit sheepish.

"Well..."

"What? What did you do?"

"Well, he wasn't going to give them up lightly. He fought pretty hard."

"You got into a fight?"

"No, *I* didn't," then she looks even more sheepish, "but my brother and his friends did." She grins. "But I got them back for you..."

"Was anyone hurt?"

"Let's just say that Zak's got another black eye to match the one he's already had."

"No!"

"Yep."

I stuff the panties into my bag, and nothing can douse the feeling of relief that's flowing through me, knowing they are safely hidden in the bottom of my school bag. Never again, never. I will never let myself get into such an embarrassing, humiliating situation again. I'm just so grateful that my father will never know just how much I let him down.

I've never been more thankful that school is out for the day, and as Linda goes off to the gym to practice for the cheerleader try-outs, I walk along the halls alone. I'm deep in thought, planning how I'm going to dispose of my panties, for I'll never wear them again...I think I'll cut them up into lots of little pieces and flush them down the toilet.

I'm pushed and jostled along with a tide of kids

all set on getting out of the building as quickly as they can, and as I'm swept along, I hear the principal shouting, but I can't see who he's shouting at. Suddenly there's a space between the kids and I see Zak—with two fresh black eyes, and his friends, all with red marks and cuts on their faces—sitting uneasily next to Linda's brother and his friends, with no bruises, but all are downcast beneath the principal's anger.

"Tell me! Who started this?" he demands.

"They did," Zak spits out venomously. "You wait 'til my dad sees what you've done to my face."

I'm rooted to the spot, suddenly terrified that Linda's brother will reveal the reason for their fight.

Linda's brother says sweetly, "They started it, sir; they were rude about my sister and my mom."

Zak scowls but says nothing. He can hardly turn around and say that he had my panties and was threatening to send them to my father.

"What have you got to say for yourself, Zak?"

"We didn't mean anything," he says, defeated.

"Well, you'll all have detention for a whole week and I'll be writing to your parents. I will not have such behavior in my school."

I stand and listen as the crowd splits past me. The principal turns and goes back into his office. Zak sees me standing there, watching his humiliation.

"Slut," he hisses under his breath, but I hold my head up high and walk on, while he and Linda's brother and their friends head towards the detention room.

I'm deep in thought as I walk home. What if his parents are mad that he got hurt at school and try to find out what it was all about? Even though I have my panties in my bag, am I really safe? Is this really over?

My stomach churns as I think of it all being dragged up again, but then a thought pops into my head that calms me. If Zak's dad gave him his first black eye, he's hardly likely to go to the school to complain that his son got into a fight; and if Zak told him the real reason for the fight, he might beat him again. I'm relieved as I think it through, but I also feel a little bit sorry for Zak that he has such a bully of a dad, and suddenly mine doesn't seem so bad...at least he's never beaten us.

I'm so grateful to Linda and her brother; I'm indebted to them. I don't really want to think about the details of what happened because I know that what they did was wrong. I know that it's never right to use violence to get what you want, but as my heart soars with relief, I'm grateful that they matched Zak's vindictiveness, even if it was with their fists. Suddenly I realize that life, and right and wrong, isn't as clear as night and day.

Mom's home and she's pleased with me again

for coming straight home. I give her a hug then run upstairs to log onto my computer to send an email to Linda. My fingers are tapping hard and fast as I thank her and tell her to say "thank you" to her brother, who now has to suffer detention for a whole week because of me.

I sigh heavily as I send it and sit back, thinking about how I should get rid of my horrible panties. I can't just get rid of them in the trash in case Mom or Dad sees them and asks why I've thrown a perfectly good pair of panties away. After all, in their day they only ever owned one pair of underwear...gross.

I go downstairs and rummage through the kitchen drawers until I find the scissors. Then, hiding them up my sleeve, I go back upstairs, trying not to disturb Mom who's watching television while the dinner cooks.

I go into the bathroom and snip the bright pink panties into hundreds of tiny pieces and watch them fall into the bowl, like roses cast upon the ocean in memory of lost innocence. I stand there for a moment watching the pink tips saturate and sink to the bottom, and then, sedately, and with determination to rid myself of Saturday night and all the hurt and pain I caused and that was done to me, I flush and they're gone.

And that's the end of it.

# Chapter Four

Only that's not the end of it. My period doesn't come. I barely notice because I'm so distressed at being grounded and with Zak, who never misses an opportunity to put me down.

The only time I feel safe is when school ends and I can go home, because Zak's got himself into more trouble and is still in detention. I'm reluctant to tell Linda that he's still picking on me because I fear that she'll set her brother on him again. Although I want him to go away and leave me alone, I don't want him beaten up, so I say nothing. I also can't tell her that my period hasn't come. I'm so panicked and in denial, that I block it out of my mind the best I can.

Not being able to tell her these things makes me feel lonely, and I hide how I'm feeling when I'm with her and hope that she doesn't notice; she thinks it's all over. She doesn't seem to notice anything because Zak doesn't pick on me when I'm with her; he's not stupid. It hurts because I didn't ask for all this. I liked him...a lot, and I was as angry as he was that my dad tattled on him to his parents, but it's all gotten out of hand and he obviously blames me, yet I had nothing to do with it and have been as hurt as much as he has.

As I walk along the hall towards the exit, I pass the notice board and a bright orange flier catches my attention. "If you can run, run for us. Join the school running team and let's be winners."

I wanted to join the running team but I thought all the places had been taken. Excitement flashes through me but it's doused almost immediately when I remember that I'm still grounded. Then another flier announces that there are still some spaces for trampoline club, too. I wanted to do that as well. I decide to get Jacky to help me make Mom and Dad lift my grounding so that I can join in.

She's already home when I get in, so I drop my bag and go upstairs, knocking gently on her door.

"What is it? Are you all right?" she asks with concern on her face.

"I'm fine," and then I plead with all my heart, begging her to help me.

"I'll try, okay? But you'd better be ready to agree to anything."

"Anything," I say, meaning it.

I start my homework with one ear listening for Mom and Dad to get home, and after an hour they're both downstairs in the kitchen chatting about their day. I stay upstairs, determined to finish my homework so that they'll be pleased with me and see that I'm trying to do better. It's hard, though, because I'm having trouble concentrating. I want to join those clubs, I want to belong and have fun with other kids. I want to run for the school and win trophies...I know I can do it. My hopes were dashed when my parents grounded me and I figured all the spaces were gone, but now that I see they aren't, my hopes are all fired up again. They have to let me...they just have to.

"Dinner's ready," Mom calls.

Jacky and I meet outside my room. "Let me handle it, okay?"

We sit around the table. I'm anxious and fidgety.

"Did you finish your homework?" Jacky asks.

"Yes. I had three pieces of work to do. They're not due until next week ,but I thought I'd get them out of the way, then I can work on my project over the weekend." I hope I'm not overdoing it.

"Cool," she says.

We start eating and I wonder what she's going to say next. My appetite's gone.

"I've been cleaning out my cupboards today... what a mess. I've got so much stuff. I came across my swimming photos and my medals. D'you remember that, Dad? I was Hannah's age when I managed to get on the swimming team and we won the inter-school competitions. It's really hard to get accepted into the school teams; it's really competitive. Do you want to take up swimming?" she asks me.

"No, I prefer running; I'm good at running." I resist the urge to say that the hardest team to get into is the cheerleaders like Linda's trying to do, but I add, "I'd love to be on the trampoline team, too. I wish I could bring a medal home like you did."

I glance at her and stifle a grin as I see her eyes focused steadily on me telling me to be cool and not to overdo it.

"Well, can't you join those teams, or at least try out for them, or are they already full?"

"Yeah, you have to try out, but they're not full. I saw a flier today saying that they still have spaces."

I don't know what to say next because I already feel as if I've gone too far. There's something go-ing on around the table. Glances flash from Jacky to me, warning me, and glances flash from Dad to Mom, and all the time we're playing with our food, scooting it around the plate aimlessly.

Dad coughs, and I think he's choking on a pea, but no, he's trying to find a way into the conversa-tion. I think the mention of medals hooked him.

"Um, there's spaces left, you say?"

I act dumb. "Pardon?"

"Are there still spaces on the running team and the trampoline team?"

I put my fork down and look at him, feeling a bit ashamed because I know that we are manipulating him, and I hate that it feels so easy.

"Yes, there are still spaces on both teams, but I can't try out because the practices are after school and I'm grounded."

Jacky shoots me a look, and I don't know if I've gone too far.

He coughs again. Mom seems to sense what's going on and helps him find a way so that he can change his mind without losing face.

"She's been really good, dear. She comes straight home and does her homework right away. I think she's learned her lesson, I really do."

"Pass the salt," Dad demands, seeking some breathing space so that he can get ready to back down.

All three of us watch him sprinkle his dinner as a muscle in his jaw twitches.

"Have you learned your lesson?" he barks at me.

I nod. "Yes, Dad. I learned it on that night. I promise I'll never do anything like it again."

"Okay, then you're not grounded anymore. You can try out for the teams, all right? But from now on I want you to be honest with us and tell us where you're going." He puts his fork down and suddenly he looks wretched. "I only want what's best for you; I only want to protect you."

I feel bad, and Jacky and I glance at each other, a look that says we understand our dad. He loves us and is only rigid at times because he's afraid for us, and unsure of himself as a father, not having had anyone to show him how to do it properly.

Later that evening I sit on Jacky's bed with her and we watch television.

"Thanks," I say, meaning it. I find it so hard to believe that a couple of years ago we hated each other, but now she's the person I love the most in my life.

"It's okay, babe, you did it. You've shown Dad that you can do as he asks, that you can focus on your studies and show him the respect he needs."

She hugs me and I hug her back.

I go to my room and pad around in my fluffy slippers until I get under the covers and wait for sleep to settle over me, but it doesn't come.

My mind is full of jubilation that my grounding has been lifted and I can live my life again, and full of excitement that I can try out for the running and trampoline teams, and without being vain, I know I'll get in because I work hard...but something's wrong. Something is troubling me, eroding my sense of celebration, something pervasive, a shadow. As I toss and turn in denial, my mind sifts through the manipulation of my dad and what I'm going to do for the "try-outs," but I can't deny it any longer, my period hasn't come.

I'm only fifteen and our teacher says that it can take several years for a girl's period to become regular, but I started mine at the age of twelve, and they've always been regular. My teacher also says that stress can interfere with your periods, and heaven knows I've been stressed over the past couple of weeks. But even as I placate myself with excuses, I know the truth. I haven't had my period because I had sex with Zak, and that means I'm pregnant.

I can't be. I just can't be. It can't be true. It isn't true. I torment myself with fearful themes of "what ifs" until the dawn peeps through my curtains, and I drift into troubled sleep for an hour before my alarm clock wakes me, unaware that I've not slept from ten o'clock until six.

I'm exhausted and weighed down by fantasies that leave me shrouded in dread. Mom pours me cereal and tells me to "Eat up." I can't. I'm anxious and preoccupied. I check my diary to see if I've got it wrong—but no, there's a cross on the date of my last period...there's no doubt, I'm late.

I go off to school and force myself to think about the try-outs. I'm going to join those teams if it kills me. I try to ignore Zak and his friends, who continue their persecution of me, as I walk up to the notice board and sign up for both teams. They follow me but still I hold my head as high as I can and make my way to class. It hurts; it wasn't me that hurt Zak. I didn't do anything, so why should I have to deal with this?

His face is black and blue as his bruises come out, and I'd feel sorry for him if he'd only stop being hateful to me. I can understand him being mad at my dad and his parents, but why take it out on me?

I'm sick of being called a "slut." I'm not a slut. I was a virgin on that night. I feel so angry with him, but I feel even angrier with myself; I gave him my virginity.

During lunchtime I go and register with the running and trampoline clubs, and they seem really pleased that I want to join them. By the end of the day they tell me that I'm on their teams, and I'm over the moon...ecstatic.

Linda slips her arm through mine and says, "I'm so glad your dad gave in. I wish I had a sister like yours. Let's go to the mall after practice today."

She's still practicing for the cheerleader try-outs and will finish the same time I get off the running track. My face falters; I know that although my dad has lifted my grounding, he still doesn't want me to hang out with Linda. I stutter because I don't want to hurt her feelings.

"No, I can't. I want to but I'm going to go straight home."

She looks disappointed, so I say quickly, "I want to show him that I can do good; then he'll trust me again."

"I'm sorry I got you into trouble," she says. "I just didn't think he'd let you go to the party if I told the truth."

I wish I hadn't gone, I think sorrowfully, but I don't say anything. I venture to ask a question that's been on my mind since the day of my cousin's wedding.

"Why *did* you lie to my dad?"

She looks upset and I wish I hadn't asked her, but she answers and makes it okay.

"If I ask my mom and dad for anything, *anything* at all, they'll say 'No' almost before I've finished asking for it. It's like they don't know how to give, or as if by asking I'm taking something away from them. It's weird, and I don't understand it, but I know it's true and always has been for as long as I can remember. It means that if I want something, I can't ask for it outright, or be honest about it, I have to manipulate to get them to think that I don't want it; then they'll let me have it."

I look at her with a frown on my face. "That sounds really complicated. Why can't you just ask for what you want?"

"I don't know. Mom tells me that her mom and dad were really mean to her when she was little...I don't know if that's got anything to do with it."

I think about the things my mom and dad say about their parents and the childhoods they had, and it occurs to me that being a parent must be a pretty difficult job and so easy to get wrong. I know that it's hard to be the kid of someone who's had a hard time themselves as a kid. Life feels very complicated.

After school I go into the locker room and change into my shorts. I'm excited. I've longed to be on the running team so that I can win medals the same as Jacky did when she was my age.

The coach orders us to do thirty jumping jacks to warm up, and I can feel my heart racing as I jump up and down, but it's not just because of exertion, it's because I'm excited at being chosen for the team. I'm going to work really hard to be the fastest runner in the school. Dad'll be so proud, as proud as he was of Jacky when she won her medal for swimming.

The whistle blows and I tear around the track, alone on the far side except for my ragged breathing, then I race past the coach who snaps his stopwatch as I pass him.

"Not bad," he shouts, as I sail past him unable to stop. I'm bent double, panting for air, my fingertips making marks on the inside of my thighs. Some of the girls run over to me and pat me on the back, telling me that I did good, and it feels wonderful to be wanted and accepted.

I finally get my breath and sit on the sidelines watching the next girl fly around the track, and I listen to the rest of the team talking about beating the other schools in the state. I'm going to help them win, I am, I want to be the one that everyone leaps on and goes crazy with for helping them win. I want the team to think I'm great and I want the adoration that goes with being the one to win for your school. I want the adoration from the boys too, because everyone knows that kids who get onto teams have the pick of the boys. I guess that's why Linda's so desperate to be picked for the cheerleader team, and I understand.

As I sit on the sidelines and the coach shouts, "Gotta do better than that next time," to one of the girls, I feel the competition in the air; to be accepted and thought of as "cool" you have to be better than the next person. I'm determined that I will be, but as I think it, I feel uneasy. I've always tried to be as good as my sister and I know I never can be, and deep within me is a longing to be accepted for being me, just me, without having to earn medals, or to be better or faster than anyone else. It all feels wrong somehow.

Goosebumps shiver across my arms in the sunshine and I shake myself and begin cheering for the next girl who soars past the coach, who shouts, "Good job."

There's a group of kids standing on the outside

of the fence and instantly I know it's Zak and his friends; his detention must be finished.

Anxiety races through me and I pray that he won't start yelling bad things about me that will make my new team friends hate me or think I'm a slut. I turn my back to them and start talking quickly to the others around me, asking them about inter-school competitions and how it feels to run against other teams. I'm grateful that they're nice girls who want to talk to me, and as they tell me all about last year's final, I glance over my shoulder and see Zak and his friends walk off, bored when I don't seem to be bothered.

He'll never know how bothered I am, though, because he's in my head every minute of every day. How can he not be? I haven't gotten my period. My life seems to center around checking my panties for spots of blood, and every time I do, which is every time the bell goes for the next lesson, and every half-hour at home, I can't think of anything else.

"Are you okay?" Mom asks.

"What d'you mean?" I snap.

"I don't mean anything," she says. "I just notice that you keep going to the bathroom. Have you got a sick stomach?"

"No...I've just been drinking a lot, that's all."

And still my panties are clean and my desperation is renewed each time I look. "Come *on*," I hiss to myself every time I go to the bathroom.

As the days go by I'm dragged into a deep, dark pit where my thoughts revolve around what's happening in my panties. I excuse myself from class to go to the bathroom throughout the day, and Linda asks me if I'm all right.

"Yes," I say too quickly, and she looks at me quizzically, which I choose to ignore.

I can't sleep, because although I try to force my brain to focus on my running and the amazing feeling of jumping and projecting myself high above the trampoline, the same thought keeps drowning all the others—my period still hasn't come.

As the morning arrives with me having tossed and turned all night, I look in the bathroom mirror, and I'm dismayed at the bags under my eyes. I look old and I'm only fifteen.

"Hannah, your eggs are ready," Mom shouts up the stairs.

I don't know what's happening to me for suddenly a wave of nausea washes over me and I feel as if I'm going to faint. I grab the sink, but then as a tide of bile rises in my throat, I only just make it to the toilet, and heave over and over again into the water inches below my face.

"Your eggs are ready," Mom says, knocking on the bathroom door. "They'll get cold. Hurry up."

I know that I'll never eat eggs again, for the thought of them and the smell renders them unthinkable, untasteable, unswallowable, something vile and disgusting that no starving human being would contemplate putting in their mouths. I don't know what's happening to me. I've always adored eggs, whether they're scrambled, poached, boiled or easy over. I used to eat them any way, but apparently not anymore.

I go to school and Linda says, "Hey, try this gum, it's watermelon," and she thrusts a piece into my mouth.

It assaults my taste buds, and as I begin to chew, my tongue seems to swell and I start to gag. There's nothing left inside me so I don't make a nasty mess; I just embarrass myself at the side of the road, heaving.

"Hannah, what's wrong?" Linda asks.

"I've got a stomach bug, I think. Mom's had it. I guess I've got it, too."

"You need to go home," she says, and turns me around, telling me to go home.

I feel so bad, that I do as she says without any argument, even though I know that by being home my parents will want to know what's wrong with me. I can never tell them, not ever, not today, not any day. They want me to be different from their families—all those people at the wedding who had loads of kids but weren't married.

Linda pushes me away, telling me to go home to bed and she'll tell the school office that I'm ill. I go home with tears pouring down my face.

I feel awful, worse than I've ever felt in my whole life, and it's not only because I know that I'm in big trouble, it's because my body has become a traitor to me. It feels as if it's dying on me. It doesn't belong to me and seems hell-bent on making me wish I were dead.

I've never felt so ill, not ever, and over the next few weeks I develop a relationship with the toilet as nausea and sickness are my only companions. I don't want to be near anyone for fear that they may smell my breath and the recent residue of my stomach. I can't eat or drink. I don't want to for I'm too afraid, because whatever I put in my mouth and dare to swallow I know will find its way back out of my mouth, altered by the acid in my stomach into a garbled, raw, burning mass riding over my throat and tongue, as I spit and spit to get rid of it, no matter where I am.

It's the lack of respect the nausea has for where I am and what I'm doing that gets to me. If I were in the bathroom and no one was home, I could just about cope with it, but walking to school or being in class when the urge to vomit comes over me is so humiliating and scary. I'm terrified that someone will notice and my shame will be discovered, so my whole life seems to become orientated around hiding the vomiting and trying to appear as normal as possible.

I turn up for trampoline club and change into

my shorts. I feel weak because I haven't eaten for days—I don't dare—and when the instructor tells me it's my turn, I clamber up onto the canvas. My head's spinning and the room starts spinning too, but I grab the steel frame and steady myself for a moment before climbing up over the thick elastic coils.

"Okay, remember everything you've been taught. Let's see a double backward flip, a bottom drop, a knee drop and then a double bottom drop, ending with a perfect pose that's straight and controlled. Go."

I start to jump, building up momentum, but with each jump my stomach stays behind and jolts as I land back down to meet it. And just as the instructor yells at me to do the double backward flip, nausea grips me so badly that I bounce around senselessly. I try desperately to steady myself, to stop the already spinning room from spinning any further. I hold my hands out and widen my legs to gain my balance. I'm going to throw up, I know I am, and just as I think it, so the water I drank earlier, along with the chips Linda forced me to eat, shoots out of my mouth in a projectile mess all over the trampoline.

"Oh, gross," say some of the team who are all waiting for their turn. "Yuk, I don't want to get up there now."

I come to a wobbly standstill, my arms outstretched, vomit dribbling down my chin, and as all the girls stare at me, I know I can't come back tomorrow. I can't be a part of the trampoline team even though I'm desperate to be. Tears are pouring down my face as I edge towards the gap between the canvas and the steel frame in an undignified crawl that furthers my humiliation.

"I'm sorry," I gasp between fresh urges to retch all over myself. "My mom's been sick all week," I say, as I run to the locker room to hide my humiliation, but also because the nausea is so bad that, even though there's nothing in my stomach, I'm desperate to throw up yet again.

My eyes are stinging with salty tears, and when the retching subsides and I've wiped my tears away, I allow myself to cry real tears. I'm ashamed to think it, but if I have to get rid of what's in my stomach, then I wish I could get rid of the one thing that's inside me that shouldn't be there.

I manage to get myself together enough to be able to change and get out of the locker room before the trampoline team gets back from their practice. I really don't want to hear them all go on about how I messed up their canvas or how the instructor had to clean it up so that they could carry on with their practice.

My face is red and I feel utterly ashamed of myself. I wanted to be on the trampoline team so badly, but I know that no one will want me after what happened today. Something inside my head has already accepted that I'm off the team, but what troubles me the most is how I'm going to be able to convince Mom and Dad that I'm still a part of it, and doing well. I know I can't tell them that I'm off the team because then I'll have to tell them what happened, and I couldn't bear the shame. Also if they think I'm sick, they might insist that I go to a doctor, and I can't do that.

I slink off with my heavy heart and nauseous stomach before the rest of the team bursts through the locker room doors, full of who has done the best and how they could be better. I can't face them, nor do I want to see the scornful looks on their faces or hear them go on and on about Hannah who had thrown up all over the place.

Zak and his friends are nowhere to be seen and I'm glad. I really don't think I could cope with them as well. I'm crying as I walk, as a sense of desperation and hopelessness wash over me. I know I'm pregnant, I just know it. Everyone knows that pregnant women get sick, and I've been so sick that it can't be due to Mom's stomach bug.

# Chapter Five

I find myself locked in a world where there's only me in it, for I can't tell anyone what's happening inside me. I know I should, but I just can't ever seem to find the right time to tell anyone; telling means that it'll make it seem real to me and it also means that my parents will find out. I'm terrified of what they'll say or do, because if my dad can get so mad when I just got drunk and vomited in his car, I can't bear to think what he'd do knowing that I've brought the very shame into his life that he's worked so hard to distance himself from. I've always felt that I've been a disappointment to him compared to Jacky, and I don't think I could stand to see his open disappointment in me. So with these thoughts preying on my mind, I remain locked in solitary confinement, alone except for the thing that's growing inside me.

I sit through a biology lesson with my head spinning as the teacher talks about conception and how an embryo grows. He shows us pictures, and I can't believe that that's what's going on inside me, and if I weren't so terrified, I'd think it was a miracle. Then he starts to talk about politics.

"You can see why anti-abortionists get so angry about abortions, can't you? For an embryo at twelve weeks, which is then called a fetus, is a fully formed human being—it's just very tiny and immature. To abort a fetus at twelve weeks, the doctors use a suctioning procedure, which tears the fetus up and sucks it out through a straw-like implement. It's a bit like vacuuming the uterus."

I'm horrified, and gone are any thoughts I might have had about trying to have an abortion.

The class is totally silent except for him talking. "The University Hospital has been very generous to allow me to show you one of their specimens. You can't touch it and it has to stay on my table, so make a line and you can all look."

We get out of our seats and start to line up as he places a jar on his table.

"This specimen was saved after a woman had what's known as a 'spontaneous abortion' at thirteen weeks, which means that she didn't do anything to make it happen, but she just lost her baby for one of many reasons and gave birth to it naturally."

We start walking by and some kids gasp, and

others say, "Wow," as he keeps talking.

"This lady was thirteen weeks pregnant, and you'll see that the baby is completely formed; it even has tiny fingernails."

The line moves and I find myself staring at the most beautiful but harrowing sight I've ever seen in my life. The baby is floating in what looks like water, but I know it has to be something that preserves it, and he looks like he's just asleep. He's tiny, perfect, and is smaller than the palm of my hand. He's all curled up with his knees drawn up towards his chin, the way that I sleep in bed. I can see his fingernails and toenails...it's a miracle. I feel tears prick my eyes, so I drag myself away and return to my seat, hoping that no one notices.

The bell rings, and as we walk along the hall to our next lesson Linda says, "What's wrong with you? Why're you so moody?"

I don't know if she's talking about how silent I was in the lesson or whether she's noticed anything about me that's changed.

"Nothing, my dad's been getting on me to work harder at my grades, that's all."

I hate lying to her but I can't even tell my best friend what's happening to me; telling means something will have to be done, and that means that my parents will have to know.

"Yeah, what's going on with your grades? You got an 'F' last week."

I shrug as we go into the next class, not wanting to talk, for my head is spinning with what I've just seen. Sometimes at night when the fear has been overpowering, I have tried my hardest to figure out what to do. Could I get an abortion without my parents ever knowing? I don't know, and I wouldn't know how to go about it, but after seeing that tiny, perfect baby and knowing that abortions rip a tiny human being to pieces as it's sucked out, I know that I could never, ever do it. I might have been able to as soon as I missed my period, but I couldn't do it now. I know that my baby is fully formed and must be loads bigger than the one in the jar, because it's been ages now since I last had my period.

As the weeks go by, I feel as if something horrible has taken over my body; I look different and I feel different, and I hate it. My breasts hurt badly—they're so sore—and to my horror the areola around my nipples has turned dark brown. I can't bear it if I accidentally brush my arm over them for they're so sore, and I seem to knock into them all the time because they've grown so big. I'm scared silly that someone will notice and say something, so I wear baggy clothes and stop eating so that I don't put on any weight. I can't eat anyway, because I'm still throwing up all the time. I've never felt so miserable or so frightened in all my life.

Running practice becomes torture, for as I battle the nausea that's always with me and try to run around the track, my breasts bounce up and down, and the pain is agony.

I can hear the coach shouting at me to go faster and telling me that I'm not good enough; and as I jog back to the start line with a terrible pain in my side, everything goes black. I regain consciousness with the coach shaking me and asking me if I'm all right.

I've never fainted before, and as my head clears I become frightened that he will force me to see a doctor, and then my secret will be out. I scramble to my feet and tell the coach and the team, who are all standing around me wearing worried frowns, that I've got my period and sometimes I get faint. I back away and hurry to the locker room, desperate to leave the school before anyone starts asking awkward questions.

As I walk home I know that tomorrow I will have to resign from the running team because I can't do it anymore...I'm too nauseous and my breasts are killing me even when I'm walking, let alone when I try to run. I can't afford to faint again or someone will make me see a doctor.

"Hey, slut," a voice shouts out.

I turn around, and Zak's behind me with one of his friends. I start to walk faster.

"You been eating too many doughnuts lately?" They're laughing at me. "The slut's getting fat."

I cuss at him and cross the road but they follow

me. I'm desperate to cry but I don't; I just turn around and cuss at them again with words that would make my dad ground me for a year.

They jeer at me, knowing that they've got me rattled. "Goin' to go home and tell your daddy?"

I walk as fast as I can and clench my jaws in determination. I *will* not cry in front of them. I didn't know I was capable of such hatred. I wish I could smash Zak's face into the ground into hundreds of billions of pieces...this is his fault and I don't deserve to be treated so badly by him. I hate him more than I thought it was possible to hate anything or anyone.

They finally get tired of taunting me when I don't respond to them, and only when I'm sure they've gone do I allow myself to cry.

I let myself into the house and I'm relieved that no one's home yet.

I go to the bathroom and curse that I have to go so often; it seems as if I have to go every half an hour...I always need to pee. As I look into the mirror I ask myself if I really do look fatter. What makes me look bigger is the size of my breasts—they're huge. I decide that tomorrow I'm going to strap them down so that no one will notice them, and I rummage through the bathroom cabinet to find some wide, stretchy bandages.

I tell Mom that I've already eaten and she doesn't make me come downstairs when she and Dad eat their dinner; I'm grateful because the smell makes me feel sick, and if they force me to eat, I know I'll throw it up later.

I write a letter of resignation to the running coach, blaming my falling grades and needing to spend more time trying to improve them. I figure that I'll leave the running team before I'm asked to leave because my performance is not good enough, and before they all start asking questions.

I lie on my bed when I've finished and think about what to do. I can't tell Mom and Dad that I'm not on the trampoline and running teams anymore because they'll go straight up to the school and demand to know why. I thrash out all the different ways to approach the problem and settle for the only option that I believe will work. I'll hang around for two hours after school each day and go home the same time that I would if I had been at the practices, then Mom and Dad will never know.

I lie there trying to get to sleep, but my stomach is empty and there's a strange fluttery feeling happening in my belly. There it goes again, and as it keeps happening, I realize that I can feel the baby moving. I can't ignore it or live in denial anymore as I can feel the baby that's growing inside me moving about. I feel revolted as an image of a large snake fills my head, one that's writhing about inside my uterus. I sob silently into my pillow, lost in my own fear, with no one to tell.

I know I look awful as I peer into the mirror in the morning and scrub my teeth, trying to get rid of the bad taste of hunger in my mouth. I carefully wind the stretchy bandages around my breasts to bind them closely to my chest, then I look at my profile in the mirror. They don't look so noticeable, but I can't believe how painful it is. I drink some water before heading off to school with my letter of resignation in my bag.

The coach reads it and says, "Has this got anything to do with you fainting yesterday?"

"No," I lie. "I've just been getting behind with my grades and Dad says I have to get them back up before I concentrate on sports."

"Okay," he says, and that's all; my dreams of winning a medal are dashed.

School becomes a nightmare that I cannot wake myself from, and I can't concentrate at all. I can't believe how weepy I feel—all I want to do is cry all the time, and it's all I can do to stop myself.

"What's wrong will you?" Linda demands.

"Nothing," I snap, unable to control my moodiness as the pain of my bound breasts and the unrelenting nausea shred my temper.

"All right, all right!" she snaps back before walking off, offended.

I want to cry even more but I can't allow myself to. The class files out of the door at lunchtime, leaving me alone at my desk. I can't go to the cafeteria because the smell makes me want to throw up, so I get up and walk to the drugstore at the end of the road to buy a small bag of chips. They temporarily stave off my hunger, but as soon as I've finished them my stomach churns, and I have to run to the bathroom, my painful breasts rubbing against the bandages.

I just barely make it and empty the contents of my bowels in a noisy, embarrassing blast that wounds my pride as well as my body. I vow not to eat anything again if that's what it's going to do to me.

I feel utterly weak when I go back to class and don't hear a word the teachers say all afternoon because I'm more aware of Linda, who's not speaking to me anymore. The bell rings to signal the end of the day and she gets up to leave without looking at me. I pull on her sleeve.

"Linda!"

"Oh, so you're over your little mood, are you? Well, I haven't gotten over mine. I don't know what's going on with you lately, Hannah, but you're no fun anymore. You're always moody, and you don't want to do anything; you're boring. I hear you've resigned from the running team—why didn't you tell me? Y'know, friends tell each other things like that. Well, I'm obviously not your friend because you don't tell me anything..."

She walks off leaving me stunned.

I don't know what to do. Everyone heard her and my face is burning as they all file out of the door, whispering. I feel so alone and I'm desperate to cry. All I want to do is go home and hide in my bedroom, but I can't even do that because Mom and Dad won't be expecting me home for another two hours.

What am I going to do for two hours where I won't be seen? I can't hang out in the mall because someone will notice and may tell my parents, nor can I stay at school because someone will wonder what's going on and may call my house or tell the school counselor.

I leave the building and walk through the park and find myself outside the public library. That's where I'll go. It'll be peaceful, and I won't be discovered by my parents, as they don't ever go to the library.

I'm just about to go up the steps, when an over-whelming urge to eat peanuts comes over me from nowhere. There's a store opposite the library, so I go in, and the moment I've handed over the money I rip open the packet and stuff the nuts into my mouth, murmuring in ecstasy.

"Your change," the assistant calls, as I leave the store in seventh heaven. Nothing matters except the taste, texture and smell of the peanuts, and as I stuff them into my mouth and chew like a starving person, I'm vaguely aware that I've always hated peanuts. What's going on?

I go into the library. It smells musty along with the scent of polish, and I breathe deeply, finding myself desperate to fill my lungs full of the rich aroma. My sense of smell seems alive. How come the smell of polish doesn't make me feel nauseous but the smell of cooking does? I don't understand.

I sit at a large oak table where several adults are pouring over heavy, musty books. I take a book from the shelves and open it, trying to force myself to read, but when the words blur together, I rest my head on my arms and fall asleep.

I awake when the librarian gently shakes my arm. "We're about to close, dear. You need to leave."

I feel disorientated until I remember that I'm hiding out.

"What time is it?" I ask.

"Nearly seven o'clock."

I shoot out of the chair. I'm two hours late. Mom and Dad'll murder me, and despite my bound breasts killing me, I run all the way home.

"Where have you been?" Dad demands.

"I had to get some papers from the school library after practice," I blurt out, hoping that he doesn't ask anything else.

"I called the school and they said that everyone had gone home."

"Yes, well, um, after I got the papers Tracy and

I went over them. I'm sorry I'm late, I just didn't realize the time."

He mumbles, "Well, don't let it happen again. There are all kinds of things that could happen to you out there, and your mother and I were worried, that's all. Try to be more considerate, will you?"

I feel as if I'm almost bowing with apology as I edge my way out of the kitchen doorway and go to my room.

Mom says, "Come and eat your dinner," and she gets up from the table and microwaves my plate.

I know I ate the peanuts without vomiting, and I don't know how I did, but the thought of eating makes me want to gag. I'll have to try, though, because I don't want to make them madder at me.

I don't know how I manage to sit through the meal or force myself to swallow each mouthful. If my parents weren't sitting at the table watching me, I'd have scooped the food into my pockets and disposed of it later, but I can't do that, so my ordeal continues with each bite churning around my mouth like cardboard.

They finally get up from the table and sit in front of the television, and as I head for the stairs I mumble, "Thanks for dinner."

I just barely make it to the bathroom and I heave as quietly as I can. I try not to look at the burning, chewed up mass that lands into the water in the toilet. But I can't distance myself from it, the burning taste, the sounds of my retching and the sight of it swirling around as I flush, and I'm revolted. Nausea threatens to make me vomit all over again, but I hang onto the sink and try to breathe deeply, grateful that the television downstairs drowns out my shame.

And so my misery continues as the weeks turn into months. I feel as if I'm locked in a prison, isolated from everyone and trying to maintain a façade that everything's okay, that I'm doing great at school and doing even better at running and trampoline. I become further and further embellished into the lies I've been weaving around me, as my secret becomes more obvious to me yet still undetected to those around me.

Linda sits next to Sandra now; she doesn't want to have anything to do with me, and that hurts more than anything. She says that I'm a "moody bitch" and she "can't put up with me anymore." I don't know what to say to her because, even if I tried to tell her what's happening to me, she'd be really hurt that I didn't tell her months ago, and that I've been lying to her all this time.

That's how it is with my parents, too. I just can't tell them now, the moment has gone, for to tell them would mean revealing the intricate web of lies that I have spun for months and months now, and I know that I can't face it. I don't know what to do, but I know that I can't tell.

I continue to bind my breasts and starve myself, and although my face looks gaunt, no one really notices that my belly is protruding. I can see it when I'm in the bathroom, but no one else can because I wear baggy clothes to hide it.

I watch my belly shift as the baby inside me turns over, and I still can't get the image of a snake out of my mind, and it makes me feel revolted. Occasionally a knotty lump protrudes through the wall of my belly and I know instinctively that it's a foot or a hand stretching and pushing against the confines of my uterus. There's no wonderment in it for me, though, because I'm just so terrified.

School is purgatory, as Zak never misses an opportunity to bring me down. I hate him and I also feel a sense of loathing as well, because part of him is inside my body, growing and eating off me, like a parasite, changing my body beyond recognition.

I'm utterly relieved when school's out for the summer break. At least I don't have to put up with him anymore.

When I can't control the emotions that are raging through me, I throw myself on my bed and sob until I hear my family come home, then I dry my eyes and attempt to put on my "happy-face mask."

I used to keep a journal, but I stopped right after the night of the party because I felt sure that my parents would read it to see what I was up to. I'm glad that I haven't written in it, for I don't ever want to be reminded of the torment I've endured since the party. As I thumb through the book reading about how innocent my life was and how excited I was to go to my cousin's wedding, I make my way to the calendar page. I count back, and then I do it again.

There's no doubt, it's nine months ago since my cousin got married and that means that I'm nine months pregnant, and I know from my biology classes that it takes nine months to make a baby. I'm eaten up with terror; I have no idea what to do.

As each day of the summer break goes by, I stay in my room and stare at the ceiling, praying to be told what to do.

Over and over again I battle with the urge to commit suicide; that would solve *my* problem. Okay, my parent's disappointment in me would be twice as bad as it already is, but at least I wouldn't be here to experience it. But even as I think it, I know that I could never do such a thing, because I remember how I felt when I saw that tiny fetus in the science lesson. I know that I could never willfully or deliberately kill the life inside of me, even though I've wished it dead many times.

Something seems to be wrong with my brain, because I just can't make it face what's happening to me, or to reach out for help. I can't make my brain accept that I'm hurtling towards an event where

I need adults to help me, and in my denial I find myself locked in my own isolation and despair.

Mom's calling up the stairs. "Hannah, get ready, we're going out for the day."

I groan, hoping that she doesn't hear me, and I hang over the banister, and say, "Oh, Mom, I've got a headache and I don't feel like it. I just want to stay in bed until I feel better."

She falters. "Well, if you're not well, I'd better stay here with you."

"No, don't be silly. You and Dad go and enjoy yourselves, I'll be fine; it's just a headache, that's all."

"Well, okay, if you're sure it's all right. I'll call you because Jacky's away for the weekend, so she won't be home tonight. We may be back late. I'll call you later, okay?"

"Okay, Mom," I say, trying to lift my voice to show some enthusiasm. "Have a good time."

I mope around the house ignoring the faint dull ache in my back and put a movie on, but I can't concentrate on it, nor can I get comfortable. I decide to run myself a hot bath and lie there wallowing in the bubbles that hide my misshapen body. I'm so disgusted with the way I look—my breasts are huge and they're leaking clear fluid...I wonder what it is and what it tastes like, so I run my finger over the dewdrop that forms on my nipple and lick it. It's sweet and I stifle the urge to gag.

I don't know how long I'm in the bath, for each time the water chills, I let some out and watch more steaming water take its place.

I feel funny, like nothing I've ever felt before. I feel faint, and the ache in my back is still there and hasn't gone away, even though I thought the warm water might help. As I rub myself dry, I'm grossed out by a bloody smear of mucus that suddenly appears on the towel—it's slimy and reminds me of a stepped-on snail.

I retch but there's nothing to bring up, and I splash cold water on my face to try and cool me down, and swallow two mouthfuls to take the acrid burning away. But all that happens is that I throw up those two mouthfuls of water, along with a glob of green bile. I stare into the mirror, shocked at the terror behind my bloodshot, watering eyes, when a wave of pain grips me so badly that I cling to the sink in agony. Nothing makes it go away, and as it rides through me like a bulldozer over a bed of flowers, my senses are ravaged. The moan escaping from my lips rises to a panicked scream of agony.

I try to crouch down to see if that will ease the pain as it rides around my body, starting in my back and ending deep within my belly. But as I bend over, something vile happens. Something gushes down my legs. At first I think I've just wet myself, but then I see flecks of blood streaking my legs, and the smell is disgusting.

I throw up again, retching and retching over the toilet, but then another wave of agony rides through me and I have to stand up, steadying myself by holding onto the sink, even though the retching won't stop.

I want to die; I want to die right now. Help me, God, help me. There are tears pouring down my face and the figure in the mirror cannot be me—she looks like a spectre, one that heralds death, and death is what I long for right this minute.

The wave of pain subsides and leaves me trembling all over, and then before I have a chance to slow my ragged breathing, I'm desperate to open my bowels. Oh, no, not now. I can't have anything inside me. How can the human body make waste when you don't eat anything? I don't know how, but as I squat on the toilet diarrhea blasts out of me, splattering the bowl.

I pant and gag at the awful smell, praying that it'll stop, and as I tentatively wipe myself, I have to get up and grip the sink again as another wave of agony wipes me out. I don't even have time to flush the toilet before it drags me to a place where nothing else exists except the overwhelming torture that's engulfing me.

As it ebbs, I flush the toilet and turn away from the mess swirling round and round on its way down the pipe, but then I'm forced to watch it disappear as another bout of retching seizes me.

I can't hear anything other than the sound of my own sobbing, which never leaves me; it accompanies either my retching, my pain or my terror. At times it's a ragged whimpering, like an animal caught in a trap, waiting to be devoured by a stealthy predator, but then it changes to a howl of predestined apprehension as the wave of pain begins to build like a tidal wave threatening to roar over a defenseless seashore.

As the pain builds, and there's no escaping its path, my sobbing becomes a scream of agony and I stuff the corner of a towel in my mouth to try and deaden the noise. My teeth are clenched so tightly on the fabric that when the pain begins to subside and I start to gasp for air, there are teeth marks on the fabric. Sweat is pouring from me, beads prickling my forehead, and I wipe my face on the towel before the relentless waves of agony begin to rise again.

There's an inevitability dawning over me as each wave of pain rises, rages, then ebbs, so that when I feel the pain beginning to escalate I know with rising panic that nothing is going to stop its path, and I'm going to have to ride it out. There's no choice, and it *will* happen with the same certainty as night follows day and day follows night in an endless cycle.

A sense of despair flows over me, as the pains get worse and the relief between each pain gets shorter. I'm locked in a place where I have absolutely no control over my body, for something has taken it over. It has a mind of its own, a will that won't be silenced or stopped, as if it has a destination that bears no changing or negotiation. I don't want this to happen—I'm desperate for it to stop—but no amount of my longing will change its course. I no longer have any control over my body, for this *thing* has complete control over me.

I long for death, and as the pains intensify and get closer together so that it seems as if they merge into one long, constant, agonizing convulsion, I'm vaguely aware that the screaming for God to take me is coming from my open mouth.

I splash cold water on my face again quickly before the next wave begins to mount, but it doesn't happen, it doesn't come. I'm so shocked, poised with expectancy and dread, but it still doesn't happen. What now? I'm trembling all over.

I look into the mirror. I look completely wild, like a wild animal. My eyes are filled with torment and terror, and I don't look like me at all. It's as if I don't know the person staring back at me, like she's a complete stranger to me.

Then something different starts to happen. I know I'm going to have to open my bowels again. Oh, no, not again. I twist around and jam my butt down on the toilet, praying that I'm not too late or that I'll mess myself all down my legs.

But it doesn't happen. Something deep down into my bottom feels like it's going to come out, and I remember last year when I had to go to the doctor because I got so constipated. This feels like that, as if a mass of waste is compacted to a hard solid lump that takes more effort to expel than I've got energy for. I remember how I'd sat on the toilet for what seemed like ages, straining and straining as the mass inched its way out of me, and this feels the same as that, only I know I'm not constipated because earlier I lost the entire contents of my intestines. It has to be the baby coming.

Again I don't feel as if I've got any control over my body, for it's working on its own, and I have no say in the urge to bear down and push. It takes over me, and I can hear the guttural grunts in my throat as I strain. It comes and goes, and isn't constant, and I have no choice but to just let my body tell me when to push—and tell me it does.

I'm screaming in the end, and I feel such pressure that I think my privates are going to split wide open. I can't help but put my hand down there to feel what's happening, and I'm grossed out and shocked at the same time; there's a slimy lump bulging from my vagina. I pant with shock and terror until another urge to strain takes over me. I can't stop it and have to let it ride over me, yet there's a sense of relief somewhere inside me as I heave and strain, my face scarlet with exertion.

It happens over and over as I sit on the toilet. I've no concept of time as my hand searches my privates in a wild scramble to make out what's happening to my body down there. The bulge is getting bigger and bigger, and I'm utterly terrified that I'm going to split open in two if it gets any bigger. How can a space that can only handle a tampon stretch to allow something this big to come through?

A scream escapes my throat as the pressure gets so bad, "God, make me dead," I scream, as the urge to push swamps me and turns my crazed, desperate utterings into another scream. Somewhere from afar I register that my screaming sounds like the damned being cast into hell, but I'm powerless to stop it.

Suddenly an image flashes into my mind that coincides with a fresh surge of agony—my body has exploded and ripped apart—but my screams chase the image away, and just as suddenly I'm compelled to pant. I put my hand down and the bulge is no longer just a bulge; I can make out an ear, a nose and an open mouth. I'm sobbing, I'm terrified, but I'm in awe. Almost as soon as I think these things, another wave of agony flows over me and the urge to push is overwhelming; I have absolutely no control over it and a scream escapes through my clenched teeth. But then from nowhere a powerful spasm deep within my vagina expels the baby, and I have to catch it to stop it from falling down the toilet.

I can't believe it! A thousand sensations hit my brain all at once. I'm terrified because it looks blue —dead—and as it twitches I notice that it's a girl.

Something happens to me. A life has just come out of my body. I'm sobbing, and although I don't want a baby—I can't have a baby— I can't let her die either.

I'm so scared. She's not breathing. I pull her up towards me and give her a little shake, and I'm only vaguely aware that I'm sobbing when she takes a gasp and suddenly starts screaming in life-shuddering gulps for air...for life...and begins to turn pink.

# Chapter Six

I hold her towards my stomach. I can't pull her any higher as she's connected to a cord that's hanging out of my vagina. I don't know what to do as I sit on the toilet, shocked. Another wave of agony rides through me, and I have another urge to strain.

I'm so grossed out by what comes out of my body, which is still attached to the baby. It looks like an alien; I've never seen anything so gross. It's fleshy with huge, pulsating veins criss-crossing it, and it's the size of a dinner plate.

I don't know what to do. I've got the baby in one arm and I'm trying to hold the "thing" in my other arm. I'm stunned. It seems bizarre and I can't do anything but just stare in shock for a moment. The waves of pain have stopped and I'm so grateful, yet the pain between my legs is excruciating. I watch the baby turn pale and the "thing" starts to ooze slightly, and suddenly I know that I have to cut it off. There's blood and mess everywhere all over the bathroom floor, and I reach for a toilet roll and jam it hard between my legs. I put the baby and the "thing" on a towel on the bathroom floor, and then I limp downstairs towards the kitchen to find a knife.

I'm so panicked and grossed out that it surpasses the pain I feel between my legs, and I move as fast as I can back upstairs into the bathroom. I make a loop in the translucent cord and slice through it, but when it begins to ooze blood from the baby I panic. She looks pale and I'm terrified, so I do the only thing I can think of. I tie a knot in the fleshy cord, and that seems to stop the oozing.

I find some plastic bags in the bathroom cabinet and put the disgusting "thing" into it and then double bag it, so that I never have to look at it again and it won't drip all over the bathroom floor. I wrap the baby and the knotted end of her cord into a towel and then two more to keep her warm.

The toilet roll between my legs is soaked with blood and I feel faint. The pain is excruciating, but I'm driven by an urgency not to be discovered. What happens if my parents come home now, or if Jacky decides that she's forgotten something and pops back home? I find a packet of sanitary pads and wedge two thick ones next to my torn body and slip on a pair of panties.

Despite the raging pain between my legs, I work fast; I have to clean up the bathroom. I leave the baby on my bed and she's quiet, but I can't look at her, I don't have time. I take a towel and clean the bathroom floor, scrubbing and rinsing over and over...there's so much blood and mess. I go downstairs and put the towels in the washing machine. I clean and replace the knife, and I swear that I can still smell the disgusting "thing" that came out of me as I mount the stairs, clasping my stomach.

I'm in such a state of shock that I feel divorced from my own body, as if I'm watching myself from afar. I'm driven on and on, in a state of consuming panic. I have to get rid of the evidence before Mom and Dad get back. I've lost all sense of time, and they could be home at any minute.

I don't stop to think. Thinking is a luxury I can't afford. Anyway, I'm so stunned that all thought leaves me, and I'm just driven to cover my lies.

I get dressed, not knowing what I'm going to do, but driven anyway, and I look for a bag. The only one I can find is my bright pink sports bag, so I tip my stuff out of it, ignoring the smell of stale sweat, and line it with towels.

I pick up the baby and she stirs. I try so hard not to look at her, because I can't allow her to be real—none of this can be real to me—and then I place her gently into the bag. Her lips suck at an imaginary nipple and she sleeps.

A massive lump in my throat threatens to completely suffocate me, but I can't allow it to have free reign over me, not now, and I don't know if ever.

I hurry downstairs. I have to get the baby out of the house, and I also have to take that disgusting "thing" with me, I can't risk it being discovered, so I bag it up again, twice, and place it in the sports bag by the baby's feet.

It's dark outside and I walk down the street. I have no real plan, I don't really know what to do at all, but something urges me towards the church. There's always someone at the church and they'll take the baby and make sure she lives.

As I hurry along the street, I pass a public trash can and dump the "thing" into it, glad to be rid of something so disgusting, and then, glancing around me to make sure that no one's around, I walk up to the church steps. There's a notice that says, "Ring this bell if you need help, and someone will come from the house opposite."

I leave the sports bag directly beneath the notice, glance around again, and then press the bell long and hard before leaving as fast as I can.

As I limp down the road keeping close to the bushes, I allow myself to sob. I'm just a kid. It's not right that a kid should have to experience the hell I've been through today, and my breath leaves me in ragged sobs as I stumble home.

The house is totally dark; Mom and Dad haven't returned, and a sense of relief fills me. I let myself in and start to mount the stairs, but to my horror I notice drops of blood staining the carpet on each step, so although I'm desperate to lie down, I go to the kitchen and fill a bowl with water and scrub the carpet on each step until it's clean. I scout around to make sure that there's no other evidence of what occurred in our home today; I have to make it seem as if it never happened, yet as I check and recheck, there's no way that I can ignore what happened, as my body is in agony.

I stumble up the stairs and drop onto my bed. I can feel myself bleeding really badly, and so I change my sanitary pads before getting into bed.

I don't know how long I've been asleep, but slowly the realization that I'm not alone seeps into my consciousness, and I know that Mom and Dad are home. I sit up and gasp as the pain in my privates sears through me. So, it wasn't just a bad dream.

I need to behave as normally as possible, so I know that I have to go downstairs and sit with Mom and Dad for a while. I change my sanitary pads again and notice a huge bloodstain on my sheets. I vow to get up early and wash them before my parents get up.

"Ah, there you are," Mom says. She frowns at me. "Are you all right, dear? You look really pale."

"I've had a bad headache all day," I lie. "Did you

have a good day?"

"Yes, it was wonderful. I wish you'd come too; you'd have enjoyed it."

I wish I had, too; anything would be better than the day I've had.

Dad turns on the television to listen to the local news as I sit back in the recliner.

"...Was found on the church steps. Hospital officials have named the baby Joy, and she's being cared for by hospital staff."

I freeze in terror. There before me is an image of a nurse holding up my baby to show to the world, and I can't deny that she's beautiful.

"...And what do you have to say to the mother?" the news reporter asks the nurse.

"Please, whoever you are, get in touch with the hospital because you may need medical help, and also your baby needs you. She's beautiful, she's a joy."

"Good God," Dad says. "Who on earth would be so low as to do such a thing? They don't deserve to live. That's disgusting. All human life is precious. Imagine leaving a newborn baby in a bag on the church steps. If I had my way, anyone that could do such a thing should be shot. They're lower than low, and hell would be too good a place for them."

A tide of shame rises in my throat and something irreversible washes over me. I am that person my father loathes, the despicable human being that doesn't even deserve a place in hell. As the thoughts seep through me, I'm taken to a place where life cannot be sustained, and the image of my baby on the television as nurses jostle over who's going to hold her next remind me that I have no place on this earth.

I stand up deliberately, focusing on not giving away that I'm in absolute agony, and I say, "I'm so glad you had a good time today. I'm tired now; goodbye. I love you."

"Goodnight, love," Mom says, but Dad just nods as he continues to decry the "awful human being that could do such a thing as to leave a precious new human being in a bag on the steps of a public place. What would have happened if one of the abandoned dogs that roam the streets had gotten it...?"

I don't hear anymore. The image of my baby being ripped to pieces by hungry dogs is so horrific that I leave the room with only one intention...to end my pain and to end my life. I am not fit to be alive; my dad says so and he's right, he's always right. People like me should be shot. He has always tried to distance himself from people that "do the wrong thing," yet here I am, his daughter, having done the wrong thing, not just having thrown up in his car or lied to him about a party, no, I've done something monumentally wrong.

There's no place for me here in this world. The lies I've told leave me no way back—every part of my life for the last nine months has been a lie; hell on earth. I pray that the hell I know I'm going to will be less painful than the isolation I've endured from my family and my best friend, the loss of my dreams to win medals for my school, and worse, the ongoing persecution from Zak.

I stifle my sobs as I go into the bathroom, and hovering above all the reasons why I feel so ashamed of myself for all the lies I've told is an image that refuses to leave me...my baby's face.

What have I done?

My body is ravaged with pain, and blood is pouring from me, soaking pad after pad, and all I want is out. The pain is too awful. With a calm but troubled sense of stillness, I open the bathroom cabinet and empty all the bottles and packets of pills into my cupped hand, and I watch my reflection as I swallow as many as I can with each gulp of water.

I can't stand the pain anymore, and I don't know which hurts the most: the pain in my ripped vagina, the pain of disappointing my parents, the pain of lying to everyone, the pain of Linda not caring about me enough to find out what's wrong, or the pain of having left a beautiful gift in a public place without even giving her a name or kissing her goodbye. I don't even dare to think about marauding dogs, for my condemnation is too great.

I finish taking the pills, change my pads so that I don't make too much mess of the bed (I'd hate to be remembered for the mattress my parents had to throw away) and climb beneath my sheets, my body in agony, and my heart destroyed.

• • • •

Something seeps through to me...it's pain. Am I dead? Is this hell? It hurts, but not as much as...giving birth to a baby. I awaken as the realization jolts through me. I'm not dead, I can't be because my butt hurts really badly, and as I force my brain to take in the sounds around me, I feel my breasts hurt as well.

I keep my eyes shut as consciousness swims over me because I can hear voices, voices I know, voices belonging to my parents and to Jacky.

I lie there listening, not knowing what to do; I just want it to fade away. I don't know how to be alive or to face everyone who loves me.

"Why didn't she say?" I hear Mom sob. "I can't bear to think of her going through all that alone."

I hear rustling and imagine that Jacky has just taken Mom into her arms. "It's okay, Mom, it'll work out."

Mom's sobbing, "Why couldn't she come to me?"

"I can't believe it," Dad says. "A child of mine!"

"Dad," Jacky says. "Shhh, she's moving. Please be quiet."

I'm so grateful to my beautiful sister. She enables me to surface, to become alive again, even though I don't want to face what I've done.

Mom grabs my hand, "Hannah, oh, my beautiful girl, wake up. Why didn't you tell us? Why didn't you let us help you?"

"Mom!" I hear Jacky warn.

I feel Jacky's hand in mine.

"Hannah, she's beautiful. She's downstairs in the neonatal department. Baby, why didn't you tell us?" My eyes flicker open but are quickly blurred by tears. They are around my bed, all looking at me. I feel so ashamed.

There's activity in the room, and they're all pushed out of the away.

"Okay, we need to take her now. You can follow us if you like, okay?"

I feel myself being lifted and the ceiling flashes past me as I'm propelled along a hospital corridor, only vaguely aware of my family's voices following me. I'm lifted into an ambulance and I feel the engines fire up.

A paramedic talks to me with gentleness in his voice. "Y'know, it'll all work out okay, just you see."

His voice trails to nothing for a moment and then he adds, "I saw her, y'know. You've got a beautiful baby."

He goes quiet as tears roll down my face, and as I cry he takes my hand and holds it while sobs rack my body.

I stare into space when I've got no tears left to shed, and after what seems like a very long time, the ambulance slows, and comes to a stop. The doors open and suddenly I hear a voice that I know. I'm confused; I don't know where I am, yet I know that voice.

"Hello, sweetheart," a gentle, loving voice says. I open my swollen eyes and my vision is filled with the sight of Miss Tina, and I can't stop the tears from rolling down my face again. "You're okay. Everything will be all right." She takes my hand, and I grasp it with the desperation of a drowning sailor.

I don't know if my mouth utters the thoughts I'm thinking, "Don't leave me, I'm scared," but she seems to know, because she doesn't let go of my hand while the paramedics wheel me into a building and help me into a bed.

"This is Beach Haven, you know, the place I told you about at school. You'll be all right here...we'll help you."

Miss Tina plumps my pillows and hands me a "call-bell."

Jacky walks into the room and pulls up a chair, and Miss Tina says, "Just visit for a little while, okay? She needs to rest."

"Hannah, I love you. Why couldn't you have come to me? I can't bear to think of you going through something so scary all alone."

"Dad," I utter, not knowing how to cope with his disappointment in me, after all, this is so much more serious than lying about a party, getting drunk and throwing up in his car. And suddenly I'm faced with the thought that although lies are lies, some lies seem infinitely more serious than other lies.

I wish my parents weren't here. I can't face their disappointment in me. I just don't have anything left inside me with which to battle their determination to rise above where they came from. I know that I'm a failure to them and a disappointment, but after living for fifteen years trying to make their dream of being a middle-class family come true, I've got no energy left with which to rescue them. I hurt too much.

Mom comes to the side of the bed and she's crying. Jacky squeezes my hand and glances at Dad, who looks at me with something horrible on his face.

"I'll wait outside," he says, and Mom glances over her shoulder as he goes through the door, then she rushes after him, saying, "This is so hard for him. I'm sorry, Hannah." I burst into tears.

"You'll have to give him some time, Hannah. It's been a bit of a shock but he'll get over it," Jacky says. I'm not so sure. His disappointment looked devastating to me.

She holds my hand. "Hannah, I wish you'd told me; I could've helped you. I can't stand the thought of you suffering so much on your own...being all alone for so long."

She shakes her head in disbelief and I can hear and see the pain in her face and voice. I feel so guilty.

"I'm sorry," and I really mean it, because I'm more sorry than I can possibly begin to say. "I didn't know what to do. I couldn't face Dad...I just hoped it would go away."

She tries to reassure me that it'll be all right, but I don't believe her because Dad has walked off in disgust and Mom hasn't come back. Part of me hurts badly that they have walked off—the part of me that is desperate for their approval and unconditional love. But another part of me is pleased that they've gone, for I can't cope with their recriminations, their disappointment, for I've become exactly the type of person they've tried so hard to leave behind. I've become a single mother, one who won't finish school because she "got herself into trouble," and I'm just the same as my cousins. I know Dad won't ever forgive me.

Miss Tina appears in the doorway. "Okay, I'm afraid that's enough; she needs to rest. You can call anytime you want to find out how she's getting along, but right now I need to take care of my girl."

I lie there, my body aching, and although I wasn't conscious at the time, I know that doctors must have been working on my ripped vagina; it hurts so badly that I lie as still as I can. A warm glow flows through me as Miss Tina claims me as "her girl," and although I'm sad that Jacky has to go, I'm glad that I don't have to cope with the stress of wondering if my dad is going to come back in to tell me that I've brought "dishonor" to his family. The truth though is that what's worrying Dad is that I've given the rest of his family, and Mom's, something to gloat over for years to come; it's not so much about dishonoring him.

Yes, although I don't want to see my sister go, I'm glad when Miss Tina insists that I need rest and shoos her out. I'm woozy but I manage a smile as she backs out of the door blowing me kisses.

I drift off to sleep and it's a welcome relief. I feel completely ravaged, physically and mentally, and something deep within me acknowledges that I'm just too young to be dealing with all the emotions that are raging through me.

It seems ages later when a gentle hand holds mine, and I open my eyes.

Miss Tina smiles at me. "Hello, sweet girl. Are you doing okay? Can I get you something to drink?"

She doesn't wait for an answer but goes to retrieve a plastic cup with a straw in it, and she rests the straw next to my lips. I suck, and it tastes good. It's the first taste I've had since...since I tasted the dewdrops from my breasts in the bath, and then my own bile in my throat as I gave birth.

I start to cry.

"It's okay," Miss Tina says. "It's okay. Try and sit up."

My butt hurts so badly that I try sitting on my side, but even that's no good.

"It hurts," I wail like a baby.

"I'm not surprised. You poor girl, giving birth without the help of a doctor or midwife can be very hazardous. You might have died or bled to death. As it was, you were lucky, but the baby came out too fast, without any kind of control to ease it out, and she ripped your vagina quite badly, so you've needed lots of stitches. That's why it hurts so badly. They're soluble stitches though, which means that as the tissue heals, the stitches will melt and fall away." She pats my pillows to make them nice and fat. "We wouldn't want to take that lot out with a pair of tweezers now, would we?"

She makes me laugh and I wince with pain.

"What's going to happen?" I ask.

"About what?"

"About the baby."

"She's your baby, sweetheart. What do you want to do about her?"

"I don't know," and I don't. For the last nine months I've been in such denial that I've never even thought about the thing growing inside me as being a person in its own right, nor have I given any consideration to what I should do.

She sits on the side of the bed and says slowly, "Well, you have some options. You're very young, and you have your whole life ahead of you. Being a mother is hard work, very hard work, and you won't be able to do all the things your friends are doing, like partying, and night clubbing, and dating. Having a baby is for life. You can't just put it away when you get fed up with it like you could when you were a child playing with your dolls. A baby's there all the time, needing your attention constantly, and it deserves your attention constantly, too. Your friends will go off to college or will get a job and spend their money on makeup and clothes, but you'll have to spend your money on day care and diapers; there's always something that your child will need. And it gets worse as they get older, trust me, I know. I'm still paying out for my kids and they're almost grown up."

She's scaring me; I'm too young for this. I'm fifteen, nearly sixteen, but still too young.

"Then you could choose to put your baby up for adoption, where the state will find a couple who long for a baby of their own but can't have one. They will love your baby and give it a good home, a home where there's a mom and a dad; and babies need both."

I'm not so sure that they need both, because there's a small seed of doubt in me that says if my dad weren't around, I might have been able to tell my mom that I was in trouble, but then I remember all the fun things Dad did with me when I was little.

"Adoption can bring joy to a childless couple but it can bring pain, too. Giving away your baby can leave a terrible emptiness inside you, even if you've done it for the right reasons and you know your baby will be happy. That baby will grow up and wonder forever why his mom let him go. It can be very traumatic for teenagers to learn that the parents they think are their own are not, and that someone gave them away when they were tiny and vulnerable. It's not to be done lightly, and you need to think about it carefully. Another option you could have had if you had been able to talk to someone earlier is an abortion."

"NO!" I shout, gasping as pain shoots through me. "No, I saw a tiny baby in my biology class, and I know how the doctors get rid of them when they do an abortion. They suck them out and it rips their legs and arms off and mangles their flesh so that it's small enough to be sucked through a pipe."

Miss Tina pats my hand. "You're a brave girl; you saw that while you were pregnant?"

I nod. "The teacher showed us what a three-month-old fetus looks like; I could never do that, never, ever." I feel tears flow down my face. "I couldn't tell anyone. I looked at that tiny baby and I knew what was going on inside of me, but I couldn't tell a soul. I was so scared, and I felt so bad for wishing that it would die and just come out of my body like the tiny baby I saw. I could never rip a baby to pieces just to get myself out of trouble, so I just prayed that it would abort itself."

I can't help myself—I sob—and Miss Tina sits quietly, not trying to comfort me, but just waiting until my shoulders settle. I wipe my nose on the back of my hand.

"I feel so bad," a huge sob escapes me. "My dad said that someone like me should be shot. He hates me."

"Baby, you're a brave girl, very brave. He doesn't hate you, he's shocked, that's all."

"No, you don't understand, he hates people like me, who don't do things 'properly,' the way he thinks they should be done. I've brought the very shame on him that he's been trying to run from all his life. He hates me...trust me."

I'm angry with myself for giving in to the tears that belong to my father and his ideals. I don't want to cry, so I grit my teeth and force myself to face Miss Tina. "I don't know what to do. I don't know what I think," but it's a losing battle; I cry anyway.

"Don't worry, sweetheart, it'll all be okay. This is what Beach Haven is all about, helping kids find their way. You'll work out what to do and that'll be right for you."

I sniff.

"Do you have any idea what you want to do?"

I shake my head.

She takes my hand and stares at me with a smile on her face. "It's a lot to deal with for having one night of sex, isn't it?"

I nod, and say shamefully, "I don't even remember it—I was drunk. It was my first time, too."

She just looks at me.

"I didn't intend to sleep with Zak, I just drank alcohol with my friends because I thought it was cool. It was fun, well, until I threw up everywhere, then it wasn't fun. I couldn't handle it, but Zak was not as drunk as I was and so he took advantage of me. I was sick everywhere, and I was so dizzy that I had no idea what was going on...I was only vaguely aware of what he was doing."

Miss Tina says, "I feel sad that something so special as making love was lost in a moment of drunkenness...it must have been awful for you."

I don't say anything, and we sit there, lost for a moment in our thoughts.

"I didn't feel a thing; I was drunk, so drunk that I vomited all the way home in Dad's car."

"Hm," she murmurs.

"But he had my panties...I guess I left them in his bedroom, I had no idea." I feel an overwhelming sense of injustice flow over me and I start to sob again. "He met me on the school steps the next day and waved my panties in front of everyone so that he could tell them that he'd 'had me.' He threatened to mail them to my dad. I was so scared and humiliated. I really liked him before the party but afterwards I hated him, and he spent every day picking on me. I wanted to smash his head in. I know I shouldn't have slept with him, but he shouldn't have done it when I was so drunk."

"No, he shouldn't," Miss Tina says. "How could you give consent properly if you were so drunk that you didn't really know what was going on?"

"When he threatened to mail my panties to my dad, my friend's brother beat him up to get them back, and after that he never stopped picking on me. It was hell."

I hate that I think about him, but I can't stop myself.

"Will I have to tell him about the baby?"

"Yes, dear, whether you like it or not, it's his baby, too."

This just gets worse. I don't want to have anything to do with him, he's horrible, yet I'm going to be forced to just because of a moment of stupidity nine months ago when I let him have sex with me after getting drunk.

# Chapter Seven

Miss Tina tells me that I'm in the acute wing, a four-bedded unit for kids with medical things wrong with them, and she says I'll move in with other kids my age once my pain eases. She gives me two painkillers and says, "Goodnight," patting my hand as she leaves.

"It'll all be okay, you'll see. Sleep tight."

I'm asleep in seconds and don't wake until the morning. I feel stiff and sore, and using the bathroom is agony. My breasts are really sore, too, and they are hard and huge; they're leaking everywhere. I feel so sorry for myself that I cry and shuffle back to the bed and press the bell.

A nurse pokes her head around the door.

"Ah, you're awake," and seeing me crying she says, "Oh dear, what's the matter?"

I don't seem to be able to do anything but cry.

My body hurts so much, but it's more than that. I am in a state of shock and confusion; I don't know what's going to happen. I don't even know how I survived taking all those pills.

"Y'know, lots of new moms get the 'baby-blues.' It's very common to feel weepy for no real reason after you've had a baby; it's got a lot to do with your changing hormones and the emotional changes you have to make. After all, there's not just you to think about anymore, you have somebody else that is totally dependent upon you. It can be pretty scary."

She goes over to the window and opens the blinds as she talks.

"I remember when I had mine—and I was a lot older than you are—I sat and howled for days, and I felt really guilty because everyone was so happy, and so was I inside, but I just couldn't stop crying. Having a baby is quite a shock to the system. Your body will never quite be the same again, and your life will never be the same again, and all that happens to you even if your baby's planned."

She comes over to the bed and sits on the edge of it and looks straight into my eyes.

"Think how much more traumatic it is for you after the experience you've just been through. It's no wonder you're crying. How's the pain?" she asks, seeing me wince.

She runs me a bath and pours loads of salt in

the water. As I lower my raw butt into the warm water, I feel as if I'm the main ingredient of a soup, as I wallow in the salty water and waft it over my wounds. She walks into the bathroom and hands me two more painkillers, and I lie there finally feeling some relief.

I'm horrified by my breasts, they've gone mad. They'd look better on the underside of a cow—they're huge and they hurt like crazy, and they're leaking badly.

The nurse helps me out of the bath, and I feel a bit shy because I've never been naked in front of anyone before, but I can't get out of the bath without her helping me. She gives me pads to put inside my bra so that I won't ruin my nightshirt, and then she hands me a sanitary pad.

"I usually use tampons," I say.

"Oh, no, not now. You can't use those for at least six weeks after having a baby, not until the postnatal check up with your doctor. But in your case, where you've got so many stitches inside you, it'll be a lot longer. If you insert anything into your vagina you run the risk of getting an infection, so just keep the area clean and change your pads regularly, okay? Oh, by the way, you've got a visitor."

She leaves the room, and I can hear her chatting away to someone as they come down the corridor.

"She's in there."

I look at the doorway wondering who it's going

to be, and I can't believe it...it's Linda. I burst into tears and she rushes over to me, throws her arms around me and cries, too.

"I'm so sorry I wasn't there for you, Hannah. Why didn't you tell me? It was the night of the party, wasn't it? It's all my fault for taking you there and giving you alcohol. I'm so sorry," she gushes.

We hold each other and I feel overwhelmed with love for my friend.

"I've missed you so much," I say. "I'm so sorry that I didn't tell you. I was so scared that I didn't know how...I kept praying it would go away and then it just became harder and harder to tell anyone because it meant admitting I'd been lying all the time."

I grab a tissue and blow my nose noisily.

We engage in a strange "dance" where each of us tries to take the blame and excuse the other, and in the end we stop and just stare at each other, smiling.

"You know, you're the hot gossip at school; everyone's talking about you."

I feel a moment of dread, but then I notice that's she's grinning.

"Yeah?"

"Yeah! And guess who's gone very quiet?"

"Zak."

"Yes. He came to school yesterday with two black eyes."

"Why, how would his parents know he had anything to do with it?"

She grins, and I can see that she's enjoying herself.

"Rumor has it that your dad went over to their house and punched both Zak and his dad in the face."

"No!"

"Yes. I figure that one of those black eyes was from your dad but the other one was probably from his own dad."

"What happened?"

"Zak's dad called the police and they arrested your dad."

My stomach churns with anxiety.

"He has to go to court."

"No!" Thoughts are flying around my head as I hear her enjoying herself recounting the gossip that's spreading through the school. I can't believe that my dad would do such a thing; he hates people that fight. It dawns on me that he's no better than his brothers, who he despises for fighting and not being able to control themselves. Suddenly he's the same as them, and he wears the same shame as I do. I should feel triumphant but I don't, I just feel sad and guilty. He wouldn't be in this position if I hadn't gotten pregnant and shamed him.

"What was he like towards you?" Linda asks.

"Hateful, but I don't blame him. He walked out

of here last night; it hurt, but I guess I deserved it."

"Hannah, you *don't deserve* anyone being hateful towards you. That reminds me, what are you going to do about Zak?"

I remember the conversation I had with Miss Tina last night. "Miss Tina says that he has a right to know his child. I hate it...I hate him after all he's done to me all this time, but she says that I don't really have a choice."

"That sucks."

"Yeah, it does."

"What are you going to do? Are you going to keep the baby?"

I shake my head. "I have no idea what to do. I haven't even thought about it. I don't know if I can; I mean, I won't be able to if Mom and Dad don't agree. If they say 'No,' I'll have no choice but to put her up for adoption."

"Have you seen her?"

I shake my head.

"Only right after I'd given birth to her, but then I didn't really look. I didn't want to. I didn't want to accept that it was happening."

"Oh, Hannah, I'm so sorry I wasn't there for you. I can't stand to think of you hurting so much, for all that time, and me being such a bitch. I promise that I'll be there for you all the time from now on."

We hug again, and a sense of stillness comes over

me as she chatters on and on about everyone talking about me at school, and how everyone knows that it's Zak's baby.

She's laughing, revenge rolling off her tongue. "You should hear everyone call him a rat as they walk past him. Now he knows what it's like to be picked on all the time, and he doesn't like it."

I understand why she's smiling, and I hate feeling this way, but I'm glad that he knows how painful it is being picked on all the time. Perhaps now he'll stop.

"You'll be the prom-queen when you come back to school. You *are* coming back, aren't you?"

"I don't know. I don't know anything," and as I say it, I realize that my whole future depends upon what my parents decide. They may decide to kick me out and send me to live with one of their relatives, the ones they disapprove of so much, or they may say that I can stay at home only if I give up the baby. There are so many "ifs" and "buts" that I just can't answer her.

An aide brings me a milkshake, and it feels so wonderful to suck on the straw and not be worried that I'll throw it back up again. It's also great to actually be able to eat and satisfy my body's desire for food. I've starved it for nine months, but now I can give in to its urges to be satiated and full.

"It's time for you to go," the aide says to Linda. "You've got another visitor, Hannah."

Linda hugs me hard and vows that she'll never leave me alone again, no matter how moody I might seem, she says with a grin across her face.

"Come on in," the aide says, and my mom steps into the room, her face an apology.

"Hannah, I'm so sorry I walked out last night. It's been a difficult few days, and Dad's having a hard time coping with it."

I speak quickly, not really knowing what to do with my shame. Linda has reassured me that the kids at school are cool with what's happened but that doesn't mean that my parents are, and they're the ones that matter to me. How they are and what they decide will determine my future, and my baby's future.

"Mom, I'm so sorry. I just didn't know what to do. Every time I went to tell you, Dad would start talking about how much he hated his family and how glad he was that we aren't like any of them, so I just couldn't bring myself to tell you. I know I should have, but I just couldn't find the right time. How do you find the right time to tell your dad that you've let him down, and that his family is now the same as the family he disapproves of so much? I'm so sorry, Mom."

"I think that's why he's having such a hard time coming to terms with what's happened," Mom says. "He doesn't know how to face his family after he's always tried to be better than them. What's happened has forced him to realize that he's not so different from them, or that's what he thinks. But he's wrong. There's nothing wrong with having standards, and he's got great standards. I think he knows our families so well that he expects they'll feed off this forever to justify their own lack of standards. Your dad has standards, Hannah, and he's right to have them, but he needs to learn how to rise above our families' constant arguing and trying to put each other down. It's not going to be easy for him, but he loves you, so he'll make an effort, I know he will."

"Mom, what am I going to do?" I ask.

"You're going to get better and come home, that's what you're going to do."

"I want to come home, but what's Dad going to be like? I feel bad enough about what I've done without Dad picking on me all the time. I've had nine whole months of Zak picking on me constantly after Dad told his parents about the party, and I can't cope with anymore."

"Dad has some growing up to do, and so do I. I'm so sorry, Hannah, that you didn't feel able to tell us. It's hard being a parent sometimes. You'll understand when your daughter grows up."

She's talking like she's already accepted the baby.

"What am I going to do about her?"

"You're going to bring her home, and I'll help you as much as I can. We'll work it out. You can't let her go, Hannah, she's here now and that means that she's a part of this family. I couldn't cope with knowing that I had a grandchild living with strangers, believing that we didn't want her."

I start crying all over again as her words sink in, and I understand what they mean to me. I'm going to be able to keep my baby—I'm a mother, and my mom's a grandmother. She holds me and we cry together.

"Try not to worry about Dad; he'll be okay."

She stays for a while until I get sleepy; then she kisses me and leaves, saying that she'll be back.

The rest of the day floats in and out of my consciousness as I keep dozing off to sleep; I can't believe how tired I feel. By the time the evening comes, my breasts are in agony.

Miss Tina pats my hand as I cry.

"I know, it's tough at first. Your milk's coming in. It takes a while for it all to settle down. Eventually, when the baby takes what she needs, you'll only make the amount of milk she needs and no more. But until it settles down, it can be painful and distressing. What we have to do is to pump some of the milk off, which will ease the feeling of fullness, and then if your breasts are still sore we can apply some hot washcloths, which will ease the discomfort a bit."

She leaves and comes back with an odd-looking machine, and to my embarrassment she attaches one end onto one of my breasts and then flips a switch. I wince immediately as the part attached to me sucks my nipple deep into the machine, and I can feel it pulling the fluid from me. I feel like a cow being milked, and again the thought pops into my head that I'm much too young for all this. I should be chillin' with my friends and talking about my favorite band and what shade of eye shadow suits the color of my eyes. I shouldn't be doing this; it all feels very alien to me. But I resist the urge to cry because Miss Tina's right—as it sucks the milk out of me, I feel less pressure, and it's a relief.

The milk is siphoned along a tube, and it finds its way into a bottle. It feels strange to think that my body has made something for my baby to drink, something that will make her grow.

Miss Tina sits on the edge of the bed while I'm being "milked."

"We'll just take a little off, enough to relieve the fullness. Y'know, breast-feeding is the most natural way of feeding a baby. It's what God intended. Your milk has every nutrient that the baby needs but, more importantly, it has antibodies in it that fight infection, and no formula can hope to be as good as breast milk for that reason. It's more than that, though, it's a wonderful way to bond with your baby—and that makes such a difference to the relationship you build with your child."

As she's talking, I wonder if my mother breast-fed me, but when I think it, I'm a bit grossed out, so I stop.

"It takes a bit of time to get it right, and it can be painful to start with if you don't gently build up the amount of time the baby has to suck on each nipple; but when you've got it right, it's fantastic."

She looks at me with a twinkle in her eyes. "It really is, Hannah, there's nothing like it. It's the most precious moment of your life, a closeness that you'll never find with any other human being, quite aside from it being free and always on tap—no getting up in the middle of the night to prepare formula, because it's already ready."

It feels bizarre having this conversation, when only days ago I was in denial that I was even having a baby, but I listen to her even though it all feels odd.

"I also think it'll be good for you to breast-feed because you've spent nine months wishing your baby would just disappear, and that's bound to play on your mind and leave you with feelings of guilt. Breast-feeding will help you get past those feelings, for you'll be doing everything you can to keep your child healthy and to keep her alive; those feelings will cancel the others out. Okay, that's enough," and she unplugs me.

As she wheels the machine out of the room, she says, "Oh, by the way, you've got a visitor."

She comes back with Jacky, who's holding my baby in her arms. My stomach does a double flip, and Jacky's grinning.

"Here she is, Hannah, she's beautiful," Miss Tina says, and Jacky hands her over to me gently.

I can't believe it. My baby's here, no longer stranded in a sports bag, wrapped in towels and feeling hungry. As I look at her and she snuffles, I forget the pain in my butt and breasts; everything ceases to exist except for this perfect human being nestling into my arms.

Something very strange happens to me; I can feel my nipples tweaking and an urge comes over me...I have to put my baby to my breast, to allow her to suck. I don't know where the urge comes from and I don't care, I just do what feels natural.

Miss Tina helps me to position her so that she can get as much of my nipple into her mouth as possible and she clamps onto me with the desperation of a drowning man and I understand. I felt the same desperation yesterday, or was it the day before, I have no idea. She sucks and sucks in order to sustain herself and to form the attachment that was destroyed the moment I cut the cord, and I marvel at her determination to cling to life.

Jacky has tears in her eyes and so have I, but we laugh through them.

"Oh, Hannah, she's so beautiful, I can't believe it."

I take my baby's hand, and she coils her tiny fingers around one of mine and grips so tightly that I giggle. She's not going to let me go, and briefly I wonder how I could ever have thought about letting her go. I know that no matter what happens, I'll never leave her again, ever.

She makes little snorting noises as she sucks, and I stroke her face, taking in everything about her—her tiny perfect fingernails, the creases in her ears, her wispy dark hair and tiny little eyelashes. She's a miracle.

She falls away from my breast, a dribble of milk oozing from her rosebud lips, sound asleep and full, and we look at each other and smile with the wonder of it all.

"She looks like Dad after eating a pot roast," Jacky laughs.

"How is Dad?"

"He's quiet, very quiet. It was Dad who found you, and he was beside himself."

"I know he must have been angry."

"Not angry so much as terrified, I think. He says that he opened your bedroom door, something he never does, to check on you, and it was only because you were bleeding so much that he saw a stain on the sheets. If he hadn't seen it and just thought you were asleep, you'd have been dead by the morning from blood loss, let alone the overdose you took."

A tear runs down her face.

"Hannah, I couldn't have handled it if you'd died. What would I do without my little sister? I think Dad was really shocked because he doesn't know what made him check on you, and I think he's frightened at just how close you were to dying. Nothing's ever so bad that it's worth dying for. Promise me that if you ever feel that much despair again you'll talk to me, or if not me, then someone else. Promise me, Hannah."

"I promise, and I'm so sorry. I just didn't know what else to do, and when I saw on the news that my baby had been found and I heard the terrible things Dad said, I just couldn't see any way out. I'd thought about committing suicide while I was pregnant, but I knew that I couldn't kill the baby inside of me. But once it was out, then I felt that it would only be me that I was killing."

"But, Hannah," she says, with a wail in her voice. "What about us? We all love you so much. How could we have ever coped without you? Killing yourself may have stopped your own pain, but what about ours? Ours would have gone on for the rest of our lives. We'd have each been left wondering if it was something we'd said or done, or something we hadn't done that had tipped you over the edge. Although we would all have carried on, because we'd have to, I guess, none of us would have ever really known true happiness because that little seed of doubt would sit inside us forever."

I'm crying now, not tears of joy anymore, but tears of shame and sadness. I can't bear that I've hurt my family so badly, but I'm also crying because the way Jacky's talking lets me know that my parents really do love me, even though I've always doubted it. I've always known Jacky loves me, but I've felt as if I'm second best to her and a disappointment to my parents after she was so good at school.

"I don't say these things to make you feel bad, baby," she says, taking my hand, "I say them because I don't think you realize just how much you mean to us all in this family. Maybe Mom and Dad don't say it enough. I know they're constantly getting on you about your grades, but it's only because they want you to do well."

"I'll never do as well as you," I sniff.

"Hannah," she says sharply, "you are your own person; you can shine at other things, you don't have to follow me. Find what it is that *you* want to do, then go for it."

"That's easy to say, but when Mom and Dad are constantly comparing me to you, it's not so easy to live with."

"I know, and they shouldn't do it; I'll speak to them."

She hands me a tissue and takes the baby from me while I blow my nose. She pats her little back and giggles when the baby burps but then becomes serious again.

"I'm so scared inside, Hannah," and her face twists with pain as she struggles not to cry. "We could so easily have lost you, and this little one...I can't stand to think about it."

I blow my nose again as fresh tears fall down my face and my nose runs. I'm so lucky to have such a wonderful family, and I vow that I'm going to make it up to them somehow, although I've no idea how.

We hold hands as our tears subside, and I'm comforted by her strength, and she's comforted by my presence. She eventually lets go and says, "Try not to worry about Dad; it'll be all right. He's got a lot of thinking to do and it's not going to be easy for him, but it'll be okay. He has to learn that you're not me and that we're different, and we are good at different things. I think he's been so desperate to not be like his family that all he cares about is good grades and getting into college, and he's lost sight of the fact that there are other things that matter as much. All his adult life he's wanted to be different from his family and then, what does he do, he's behaved in exactly the same way they do by resorting to fighting. So not only is he going to have to go to court, but he's got to deal with the fact that his behavior is just the same as his family's after all his struggling to be different, and that's got to be hard for him."

"It's all my fault."

"Hannah, you didn't make Dad go over to that boy's house and assault his parents, Dad made the choice. He could've behaved differently, but he chose not to."

Miss Tina comes back and tells Jacky that it's time to leave. She kisses the baby before handing her back to me and kisses my cheek as she stands up.

"Bye, babe, take care of my beautiful niece," and I giggle because it sounds so strange.

Miss Tina comes back after Jacky's gone, and she sits on the edge of the bed.

"Are you all right?" she asks. "You've been crying," and so I tell her the things Jacky's just said to me.

"It sounds to me as if your dad measures his success as a parent by the number of good grades and awards his children can achieve, and by whether they go to college. He also seems to be living his life through his children's successes, so that would explain why he appears to be closer to Jacky, and why he'd give you a hard time about not being as bright as she is, although I don't think that's true. Try to understand that, if you fail, he sees himself as failing, and as it's so important to distance himself from his own family, he has become obsessive about both you girls being successful at school and in your careers."

"But what about *my* feelings? You make me sound

like a circus animal. I've got to perform or else I've got no value," I say, dismayed.

"Yes, I can see why you feel that way. Don't be too hard on him, Hannah. What we do here at Beach Haven is to help kids understand but not to blame, for when you understand how something has come about, there is no room for any blame."

I sit in my bed feeling glum, listening to her.

"It's normal to want to do things differently from how your parents did them, and it sounds like it was really important to your parents to give you girls a better life than the one they had. That's fine. But in being so determined not to make the same mistakes their parents had made, they've made other mistakes instead. This happens with every generation, Hannah, and I'm certain that you won't make the same mistakes your parents have made because you know how it feels. But you *will* make other mistakes and in twenty years your daughter will vow not to make the same mistakes you've made, and so it goes on."

She grins at me as I sit with my face set in a pout.

"I'll never forget the day my daughter told me how ashamed I'd made her feel when she came to tell me that she had a hairy big toe, and I'd said, 'Yuk.' So when her own daughter came to her to complain that *she* had a hairy big toe, my daughter remembered the pain she'd felt, and said, 'Oh, how wonderful. Not everyone has a hairy big toe; that means you must be special.'"

I smile at her and she giggles.

"And I dare say her daughter will feel hurt because her mom didn't do anything to make it go away. That's how it works, Hannah. All parents make mistakes. Some are serious mistakes and others, like the hairy toes, aren't serious, except to the person who feels hurt. What makes one person feel hurt may be different from what makes someone else feel hurt. Complicated, isn't it?"

"Yes," I say, feeling suddenly very scared that everything I do for the beautiful baby sleeping peacefully in my arms will be judged, as I'm now judging my parents.

"Why don't you spend a little bit of time getting to know your beautiful baby, sweetheart, and I'll come back in a little while to get her so that you can get some sleep, okay?"

She leaves and I'm left alone with my daughter. I can't believe how beautiful she is—she looks like Jacky, and I'm so pleased—and I try to chase away the thought that I'd hate it if she looked like Zak.

She's sucking her bottom lip as she sleeps and I smile. I can't believe that she came out of my body. I whisper to her and tell her that I love her more than anything, and I promise I'll never leave her ever again. I also make a promise that I'll do my best and that I won't make the same mistakes my parents have made. Then as tears roll down my face, I hold her close to me and whisper, "I only said that I didn't want you because I was terrified."

# Chapter Eight

Miss Tina comes back half an hour later and takes the baby from me.

"I'll bring her back when she needs a feed. Try and get some sleep," and as she walks out of the room, I feel a strange sense of loss.

I'm asleep in seconds and only awake when someone shakes my arm. It's still dark outside.

"Your baby needs feeding," Miss Tina says gently.

I'm so bleary eyed that it takes me a minute to understand what she means as she puts the baby into my arms.

"What time is it?"

"Two o'clock in the morning," she laughs. "You'd better get used to being awakened because sometimes it can take months before a baby will sleep right through the night."

She turns the night light on and helps me to latch the baby onto my breast properly, and then she sits and talks to me for a while.

"Night feeding is one of the hardest things about have a new baby, and because you never get a proper night's sleep, it's easy to get tired and run down. For the first few months, make sure that you concentrate on getting enough sleep. When your baby goes to sleep, try and rest, too. It'll help you to cope."

It all sounds so strange and I realize that my life is never going to be the same again; it's changed forever.

"What I used to do with my babies was to make sure that during the night feedings I gave them no stimulation at all, and then they went back to sleep easily. Keep the light very low, just so that you can see. Don't talk or play with her, just feed her, burp her and only change her if you have to. Diapers these days are so absorbent that, providing they haven't pooped, it should be okay to leave until the morning. Changing a baby wakes it up...they sense the change in temperature. Some people change their babies before feeding when they're already awake, others change them half way through, because sometimes the act of feeding will stimulate the bowel and babies often poop while feeding. You'll soon get to know your baby's habits. So if you have to change her during the night, try feeding her just a little more afterwards so that she'll fall asleep at the breast, and then very gently lay her back down in the crib.

"One of the good things about breast-feeding is that you don't have to get out of bed and go to the kitchen to heat up formula, which would make you wide awake. If you have the crib by your bed, the whole feeding can be done without you or the baby becoming really wide awake, and it can take as little as ten to fifteen minutes before you both go back to sleep. I've heard of some parents who have been up for two hours during the night, pacing the floors trying to get their babies back to sleep, and then just as they begin to drop off to sleep themselves, the baby wakes again for its next feeding." She shudders, "How awful!"

I'm trying to listen as the baby snuffles and sucks on me.

"I can't stress enough how important it is to get enough sleep during the first few weeks, because you're dealing with huge changes in your body and in your life, and how you cope with them will impact your baby and the relationship you're trying to build with her. Everything you feel, she'll sense. She'll know when you're happy and sad; babies *know* these things without words. One of the things you can do to set off on the right foot is to try and recreate the same environment that your baby's known since the moment of conception."

"How?" I ask, wondering what she's going to say.

"Think about it—being born is a real shock to a baby. It's squashed into the birth canal, thrust out into a bright light, and feels cold and hungry, which it's never experienced inside you. It's then put into a crib where it can't feel anything warm against all of its skin, like it did inside the uterus, and then it lies there in silence. An unborn baby is never hungry or thirsty because it's fed through the umbilical cord. It's never alone because it's *held* within its mother, and it feels safe and secure because the uterus holds it tightly. The mother's bowel sounds and pulse make loud noises for the baby to listen to, so it knows it's not alone. It's been described as being in heaven, so being born is a real shock to a baby. You can minimize that shock by trying to recreate the same environment during its first month. Always wrap your baby up, leaving its hands by its mouth. I'll show you how...the Indians used to do it all the time."

She takes the baby, who starts to wail, and shows me how to wrap her, and it's like magic...she stops crying right away.

"It's like an Indian's papoose; the baby feels safe and secure, just as she was inside you." She hands her back to me and I put her to my other breast. "Babies like to hear noise; they're used to it because from the moment of conception they've been surrounded by sounds, so don't leave her in a silent room, and except for the night-time feeding, as you hold her, talk to her, or sing. When you burp her, and her ear is close to your mouth, talk or sing to her. The sensation of your cheek against hers will give her the same stroking feeling that she felt as each part of her body was being stroked by the walls of your uterus next to her skin."

"How long do I have to do this?"

"Usually only the first few weeks until your baby is more used to the new sensations around her and is starting to take more notice of her surroundings. You'd be amazed at how much a newborn baby takes in during the first few weeks of life. It's truly amazing."

The baby's finished feeding and is asleep.

"Okay, can you see how feeding and sucking sends a baby to sleep? Right, gently put her on your shoulder and pat her back at the same rate as your heartbeat to help her bring up any air she may have swallowed. But more importantly it will soothe her, as her brain will *recognize* the rhythm and sounds she heard inside you when she sensed that she was safe and secure."

I gently pat her back, thud, thud, thud, and I focus on my own heartbeat, while her face is right by mine.

"Now, talk to her softly," Miss Tina says, "because the sounds will let her know that you are there, even though she's asleep."

"I don't know what to say," I say, feeling my jaw moving against my baby's soft cheek.

"Just say anything. Your baby will feel the movement and it will let her know that the connection to you, that she's always known, is still there. Don't listen to people who say that if you hold the baby too much you'll spoil it, it's not true. Babies that are left in their cribs all alone until the next feeding become irritable and anxious; they cry a lot, causing their moms to become anxious, which makes the baby more anxious.

"If a baby isn't fed when it's hungry, it will become very distressed and will do the only thing it can to call its mother...scream. You're in danger then of setting up a vicious circle. You'll become stressed because your baby is screaming, and your baby will become even more stressed because it can sense that you are stressed.

"That's why the first few weeks are so important, because the way you deal with your baby during that time sets up a pattern of how it's going to be between you both in the future, and whether the attachment between you both is secure.

"Hold your baby, whisper in her ear, sing or say *anything*, it doesn't matter what, so long as it's in a gentle tone of voice. Wrap her firmly, leaving her hands free so that she can comfort herself by sucking, and never make her wait for food. If you do all these things, then your baby should be content and secure, and the bond between you both will be very secure. She will *know* that you are always going to be there and she'll have no need to scream, or become irritable and anxious."

I have an overwhelming urge to cry, for it all seems insurmountable to me. I'm too young to be responsible for how secure my baby will feel. I had no idea how serious it would be to have a baby and to be responsible for it. I'm really scared. What if I mess up? Will she hate me when she's my age?

"It's a bit scary, isn't it?" Miss Tina says, with a twinkle in her eye that reassures me a little, but not much. "It's a big price to pay for one night of sex, isn't it?"

She smiles at me, so I know she's not being mean.

"Okay, sweetheart, let me take her back to her crib so that you can get some sleep."

I lie in my bed for some time before sleep steals over me, thinking about how determined I am to get it right. I'm going to hold my baby as much as I can, whisper gently in her ear and learn as many nursery rhymes as I can to sing to her. I'm going to pat her back, and her butt, to the same rhythm as my own heartbeat, and I'm going to wrap her like an Indian papoose to make her feel safe and secure. I'm going to do all these things so that I can get it as right as I can, even though I'm only a kid myself.

I spend the next day getting to know my baby better and I practice everything Miss Tina told me, and it's easier than I imagined, for it comes naturally. She lies in my arms and doesn't cry at all; she opens her eyes and stares at me, as if she's looking deep into my soul, and I stare back. When I blink, she blinks, and when I poke my tongue out, she does the same. She makes me giggle, and I'm amazed by her.

Mom and Jacky visit, and I show them how she copies my facial expressions and we laugh with the wonder of it all. It's amazing, but the most amazing thing is how much I love her already. I can't imagine life without her; it's unthinkable.

That evening Miss Tina comes into my room and says, "How d'you feel? Do you feel ready to meet the other kids here? I know they're dying to meet you."

I feel a bit scared and it must show on my face.

"C'mon, it'll be fine. It'll do you good to reach out to kids your own age, and tonight we're going to be talking about reaching out to people when you need help."

I lower my eyes, knowing that I should have reached out to someone, anyone, during the past nine months. I follow her in my pajamas, trying not to wince in pain as I walk, but it's not far, and as she opens a door which says "Group Room," a sea of faces looks my way.

"Everyone, this is Hannah."

They all say, "Hi," and smile.

I sit down gingerly, not wanting anyone to realize that my butt feels as if it's on fire.

A girl smiles at me and says, "My name's Candy. We've been dying to meet you and to see your baby. What's it like having a baby?"

I feel shy and don't really know what to say.

Miss Tina comes to my rescue.

"Hannah, this is a place where everyone is honest about what they think and feel. You will be accepted for who you are and no one here will be judged or rejected. You can say exactly what's in your heart and it will be okay. Part of growing as a human being is to know who you are, what your feelings are, and accepting that they are okay...we are all different but we all have equal worth."

Candy asks me again, "What's it like having a baby?"

I pluck up the courage to answer her in front of all these kids who are looking at me, demanding an answer.

"It's...terrible, frightening, and yet..."

I drift off for a moment as I remember my baby sticking her tongue out when I stuck mine out, and blinking when I blinked.

"...It's awesome."

They're all staring at me, waiting for me to say more.

"It was terrifying because I couldn't tell anyone, and even more terrifying to give birth on my own with no one to help me. It's also scary to think that another human being is totally dependent upon me, when I'm only a kid. Yet, I don't know, when I hold her in my arms and she looks at me, it's the most wonderful feeling in the world."

Some of the girls sigh, but others press me.

"But how come you didn't tell anyone that you were pregnant?"

I swallow hard and try not to cry, suddenly feeling overwhelmed with guilt.

"I couldn't...it would've killed my parents. They wanted me to follow in my sister's footsteps and go to college. They wanted us to be better than anyone else in their families."

"How did you manage to keep it from your parents? Didn't they notice that you were getting bigger?" a girl asks.

My face is burning and I mumble, "I couldn't eat, and I wore baggy clothes. They never noticed; they were too busy with my sister."

There's a huge lump in my throat, and as all the kids look at me, a tear rolls down my cheek.

"I feel I've let them down so badly."

I clear my throat. "My dad wants me to go to college like my sister, and he wants us to do well. He wants us to be totally different from his and Mom's families, because he's ashamed of them."

"Why?"

"Because he thinks they're no good."

Miss Tina speaks out, "Do *you* think they're no good, Hannah?"

I look at her. There's nothing in her face that gives me a clue as to how to respond, so I figure I should just be honest.

"No, I don't. I like my cousin Jade, who just got married. Dad was really mean about her because she was six months pregnant at the time. Mom and Dad hate their families and think they're worthless. They say that half of them are on welfare...I don't know if that's true...and I don't care if it is. I know that most of them aren't married but they've got loads of kids. My parents haven't allowed us to get to know our cousins because they don't approve of them, and they think they're beneath us. I hate it because I don't feel that way. They're my family, whether or not they're working or married."

"They sound like snobs to me," one kid says.

I feel really bad because the way I've described my parents does make them sound like snobs.

"My dad's worse than my mom," I say quickly. "Mom doesn't seem so down on her family, well, not as bad as Dad is about his family. He has drummed it into us since I was really little that he expects great things from Jacky and me so that we don't end up like our cousins..." tears roll down my face..."but that's just what I've done. He'll see me as being

exactly like the people he's spent his whole life trying to get away from."

I feel such despair that I can't stop my tears.

"That's why I couldn't tell my parents...my dad
would have freaked out, he'd have been ashamed
of me and would have disowned me. I couldn't tell
anyone else either in case they told my parents. I
felt trapped, alone and scared."

"But didn't you have any friends to talk to?" a
girl asks.

I nod. "My best friend, Linda, but I couldn't tell
her either."

"Why not?"

"Well, mainly because at the beginning I couldn't
believe that I was pregnant. I just, kind of, ignored it
and hoped it wasn't true. Then when it was obvious
that I was, I couldn't tell because something would
have to be done, and that would've meant my
parents knowing. But then..."

I swallow hard. "I couldn't tell as the months
went by because I was ashamed. Telling would have
meant that I'd been lying for months to everyone I
love."

"But in the end they knew you'd lied anyway," a
boy says.

"I know," I mumble, "I couldn't think straight. I
just didn't know what to do. It was like living in a
trap, in a spider's web where I knew I was going to
be eaten, no matter what I did."

Miss Tina says, "Y'know, everyone has troubles in their lives, that's perfectly normal. I'm not saying getting pregnant and trying to be a mother when you're just a kid yourself with all the world ahead of you is okay; it isn't. But *everyone* has troubles to deal with. It's lonely and frightening to try and manage your troubles alone. Everyone needs to reach out for support and to gain another person's point of view, because that will help you challenge the way you see things."

I think I know what she means because, until Jacky told me how devastated Mom and Dad would have been if I'd died, I'd never known. I believed that Dad would have disowned me for bringing shame upon his family, and I never stopped to think that my parents might actually care about me. They always seem so down on me when I don't make the same grades as Jacky. Success and status seem to be the only things that matter in our house...status to distance us from Mom and Dad's family. I feel sad, for my baby has their family's genes in her and yet she's perfect. It feels too complicated. We're born with all our family's genes in us, which dictate how we're going to turn out, but then we turn into something else by the way we're raised.

Candy looks sad, "You should have told some-one...anyone. It's not right that you should have gone through all that on your own. You could have died."

"Yes," the rest of the kids say.

Miss Tina smiles at me and says, "They're right, Hannah. It's awful that you felt so frightened and alone. Everyone should reach out to other people, people they trust, when they're in trouble, or when they're hurting."

The kids nod and smile at me.

I shake my head, and say, "I know, but I just couldn't because my dad would think I was scum... that's what he calls people who he thinks are beneath him." I feel ashamed.

Miss Tina says, "I'm sorry he feels that way, and I understand why you felt that you couldn't tell your parents. Y'know, all people are different but they all have equal worth in the eyes of God. To help you understand why some people believe that they're better than others, and also how important it is to reach out to others and not be isolated and all alone, I'm going to read you a little story."

She gives a little cough, and one of the girls starts to suck her thumb.

"You ready?"

• • • •

*Far, far away in the land that bobbed in and out of view depending upon the sea mist, wedged beneath a large mountain and a silvery seashore, lived a race of human beings called The Coura. The gods had made each person equal, with no* one person having more worth than another, even though they all had different talents.

Most of The Coura cared for each other and, although some were old and sick and couldn't work, those who were strong took care of those who were weak and vulnerable. Others who weren't able to hunt and fish for the villagers' food contributed to the village in other ways by making the children laugh and telling them ancient legends. They were open and honest with each other, for each person felt accepted by every member of the village. In times of trouble they had no fear of reaching out to others for comfort and advice, for each person knew their feelings would be honored and respected.

They lived peacefully for hundreds of years as the gods had intended, until a terrible winter chilled the hearts of those gentle people. Storms whipped the ocean into a frenzy so that the fishermen could not catch enough fish to feed the people, and snow forced the animals to hide in their dens to keep warm. The people were frozen and hungry, and those who could braved the raging seas and trekked up the mountain to find food. Others chopped wood, and despite their fingers being frozen to the bone, they made secure little houses to protect themselves from the fierce cold.

There was less to eat, and the piles of logs dwindled as the villagers struggled to keep warm, and as each person began to fear that there wouldn't be enough to keep them alive, something insidious crept into the hearts of those people that the gods had made equal.

One by one those who hunted for food and built houses began to band together, believing that they were more valuable than those who couldn't.

"If it weren't for us, they would starve or freeze to death," they muttered, and as they agreed with each other, their hearts became bitter. They judged each person's worth depending upon whether they could catch food or build houses, and they failed to see that some villagers had other talents.

As the winter came to an end, the gods sat and watched the villagers, the bitterness and judgment in their hearts laid bare to see. They watched as the people who thought they were important pointed their fingers at others accusingly, belittling them and robbing them of their sense of worth, and the gods became angry.

As the people openly pointed their fingers at those they believed were worthless, those villagers became fearful and ashamed, and they isolated themselves from others, lest they be rejected further. They spoke to no one and shared nothing of themselves. They ceased to be open and honest with each other, and in times of trouble they failed to reach out to others for comfort and advice, fearing that their feelings would not be honored and respected.

*The gods spoke to those self-imposed important villagers through their dreams, warning them to treat each other as equals and with respect, even though they had different talents, but the people wouldn't listen. They liked the sense of importance they placed upon the talents they had, and they liked judging others as inferior, for it made them feel good.*

*The gods tried for years to stop those villagers from judging others and pointing their fingers accusingly, but when they were ignored, the gods flew into a terrible rage and cursed the people.*

*As the people judged and berated those around them, their elbows became rigid, so that their arms were forever pointing a finger at those they felt were beneath them. When they weren't judging others or pointing an accusing finger, their arms hung stiffly at their sides. Even those who were not judgmental were cursed, too.*

*The gods were determined to teach the people a lesson in order to show them that they were all equal. As they were unable to bend their arms, they were unable to feed themselves. So to prevent themselves from starving to death each person had to kneel down on the ground, their arms stiff and useless, and bury their faces into their food like dogs. Those who thought that they were more important than the others were outraged at first, but then they knew shame, as every villager ate in the same way and at the same level.*

*The elders of the village despaired and feared that their beautiful world was doomed forever. They also despaired that the gods had deemed to punish those who already knew the shame of being branded as worthless.*

*One bright sunny day, as the sun glittered like jewels across the sea, a sailor rowed his boat towards the shore and hauled it over the sand. He walked into the village and was shocked to see all the people kneeling down gobbling their food like dogs.*

*"Good day," he said to the chief elder who had food smeared across his face.*

*The chief elder raised his stiff arm that refused to bend in the middle, and the sailor shook his hand gently, not wanting to cause the old man pain in his shoulder.*

*"I'm so ashamed," the chief elder said, his eyes downcast. "A great affliction has come upon our people."*

*The sailor followed the chief elder to his home, watching his stiff and unyielding arms hanging at his sides as he walked.*

*As they sat beneath a palm tree, the chief elder told the sailor of the days when everyone in the village was considered equal, even though they had differing talents, and then he recounted the terrible winter.*

"It was then that our village changed, and some villagers believed that they were more important than others, and they stood in judgment of others and shamed them. Since then all our people have become isolated, afraid to say what is in their hearts, to share their stories and their legends for fear of being rejected, misunderstood or ridiculed. We are like islands, alone and afraid. The gods were angry and have cursed us with useless arms so that we are forced to eat like dogs to be reminded that we are all equal."

He shook his head in despair and a tear rolled down his cheek. The sailor wiped the tear from the old man's face, as he couldn't reach his own face.

"Come," he said. "I have brought a flagon of sweet coconut cream as a gift; let us share it with all the villagers."

The chief elder felt ashamed, for he did not want his new friend to see him lap the cream up with his tongue, but he soon smiled when the sailor whispered to him as they walked back into the village.

The chief elder rang a bell with his stiff arm, and all the villagers stood before them, wondering what was going to happen.

"Follow us," he said smiling, and the villagers followed them into a park where, placed on the edge of a large round table, there was a bowl for every villager filled with coconut cream. The villagers surrounded the large table with expectancy on their faces.

A small boy rushed towards a bowl, and just as he was about to lap up the sweet liquid with his tongue, the sailor shouted, "STOP! Your chief elder tells me that before the terrible winter came, and your lives were changed forever, every person here felt valued, even though their talents were different, and that you all felt able to reach out to each other, knowing that you would be valued and accepted. Is that true?" he asked, looking around at the people who were eager to lap their coconut cream.

They muttered, "Yes."

"And is it true that after the terrible winter when some of you felt that you were more important or valuable than others, you didn't feel able to reach out to each other for fear of being discounted, rejected or ridiculed? You were all isolated and alone?"

"Yes," they said.

"The curse the gods have inflicted upon you has shown you that you're all equal, just as the gods intended, but now you need to learn another lesson. Reach out to each other. Every one of you has a part to play in this village; reach out to the persons next to you and accept them as being valuable, even if their talents and beliefs are different than yours."

*The crowd began to fidget and the sailor raised his voice.*

*"Take a bowl of coconut cream with your stiff, unbending arms and reach out to the person on your right. Hold the bowl to his lips and let him drink as a human being and not as an animal; let him drink with honor. Everyone in this circle is as important as the next person, and know that by reaching out to each other, you will never be alone and isolated again."*

*The villagers murmured in ecstasy as they drank the sweet coconut cream with the villager to their left holding it up to their lips, and they drank without lapping like a dog on the ground.*

*When they had finished the sailor said, "I don't know whether you will ever have the use of your arms again, but if you reach out to others, feed each other, share the pain you feel and let someone else help you, you'll have your self-respect and know that someone cares about you. Never suffer your afflictions alone; reach out to others, and you'll be all right.*

*The villagers smiled at each other with hope on their faces.*

*The sailor walked back to his boat, and the gods smiled to themselves as they watched the villagers reaching out to each other and accepting each other as having equal worth.*

*"They have learned well," the gods said, and*

*by the time the sailor had sailed out of sight, they lifted the curse from the people.*

*As the moon rose in the night sky, the villagers laughed and hugged each other, their arms freed of the crippling curse. They reached out to each other, and no one felt judged, alone or rejected ever again.*

# Chapter Nine

Miss Tina looks up and smiles at us.

"Okay, so this story is about reaching out to other people," she says, walking over to the flip-chart where she writes REACH OUT, then beneath it she takes the letters one by one and writes THE COURA. I smile as it dawns on me.

"This story is about two issues; the first is about equality and inequality in society, and the second is about how inequalities affect people's ability to reach out to others in times of trouble."

I shift in my chair because my ass stings; when group is over I'm going to soak myself in a salty bath.

"Before the terrible winter came, The Coura saw themselves as having equal worth—no one was better than the other, even though some were sick and vulnerable and couldn't work. Those people had other talents that were viewed as important as everyone else's. But when the terrible winter came and the survival of The Coura was threatened, the values in the village changed. The most important thing was to survive, so those who could hunt and provide food or build shelters and chop wood enabled all the people to survive. The other people's talents were still just as important, but those who had braved the terrible winter believed that their talents were better than the others. Can you think of a situation like that in our world?"

We glance around the room at each other. My mind's blank. A boy, who looks older than me, lifts his hand.

"Yes, Mike?"

"Well, it could be similar to our material world. Anyone who makes things to sell or writes computer programs could be seen as being more important than someone who cleans the streets."

Miss Tina says, "That's a good example, Mike. Cleaning the streets is vitally important for everyone's health, yet those with high paying jobs would be likely to look down on a street cleaner."

Candy speaks out. "My mom runs a day-care and she makes hardly any money, but surely she must have one of the most important jobs in the world. She takes care of the kids who will one day be the adults that will run the world we live in."

Miss Tina beams at her, and says, "Both Mike and

Candy have shown that, depending upon the values a society has at any given time, some jobs will be seen as more important than others, yet they aren't at all. Candy's absolutely right. There's nothing more important than taking care of little children, for they are the future of this world. And if we get it wrong, what's society going to be like in thirty years' time?"

"How people see status has to do with money, I guess," says Mike. "The street cleaner and childcare worker won't earn very much money but people who make things that others will pay a load of money for will seem more important."

"That's crap," a boy says.

"Randy!" Miss Tina frowns.

"Well, it is. My dad's disabled, so he works in a car park, taking tickets and giving change for the machine. That means, then, that he has no status, but he's a pastor at our church and he helps every-one. He's awesome."

Miss Tina smiles at him.

"D'you know, Randy, you have just illustrated the story perfectly. Although your dad can't compete with the big shots who make loads of money and have high status in our society, it doesn't mean that he doesn't have worth as a human being. Look at what he gives to people—comfort and guidance; how wonderful. And think of Candy's example: childcare workers love and care for our children, the children who will eventually run our world when we are old and vulnerable. Everyone has worth; everyone has something to give...everyone."

My mind is racing.

"So my cousins have worth too, even though some of them aren't working?" I ask.

"Of course," Miss Tina says.

Mike interrupts. "What does your dad do?"

Shame shoots through me.

"He's an engineer," I say. Any other time I'd have been proud, but right this minute I feel awkward, knowing that he sees himself as being better than other people, like the fishermen, hunters and builders in Miss Tina's story.

"What do your cousins do?" Candy asks me.

I shrug because I really don't know.

"Dad won't allow us to have any contact with them, so I don't know what they do, but I know they've got lots of kids."

Miss Tina says, "Hannah, every human being has worth. Whether or not your cousins earn an income is not an issue. Everyone has a part to play in this life here on earth. One of the greatest things anyone can do is to take care of children, for they really are our future. It's the hardest job anyone will ever have to do, but it's often ignored or berated. Our time on earth is so short, yet how we treat our children will impact generations to come, far more than whether we managed to sell things that go in and out of fashion."

I'm listening, I really am, but my ass is so sore that I have to shift in my seat again.

"It's like the story. Not all the villagers thought that those people who could hunt, fish and build houses were better than those who sat at home telling the children their legends and making them laugh. Those who were able to keep the people warm and enabled them to eat convinced themselves that they were more important, and that's a human trait."

"A what?" asks Candy.

"It seems that human beings have good and bad characteristics, and for an individual to see himself as better than other people seems to be a part of human nature—a bad part. It's the root of all prejudice and wars."

She shakes her head.

"Anyway, let's move on to the other part of the story...reaching out to others when you're in trouble. Before the terrible winter, when all the people still felt that they were equally valuable, they were able to reach out to everyone when they were in trouble or in pain, but what happened after the winter?"

"They couldn't reach out to others because they thought they might be ridiculed or rejected," Candy says.

My thoughts are making my head spin. I couldn't reach out to my parents because I knew that I'd be shamed and rejected.

"So, when people don't see themselves as being equally valuable, they become unapproachable. Those who feel undermined or shamed because they don't meet some high standard, feel that they'll be ridiculed. They feel as if their thoughts and feelings don't matter, so they won't share them," Miss Tina says, forcing us all to think.

"And if you feel that you'll be ridiculed, shamed or rejected if you express your feeling or your fears, what will you do?" she asks, looking around the room.

I know! "You'll be quiet and not tell anyone your fears in case you're shamed or rejected."

The room's silent for a moment as everyone looks at me, and then at Miss Tina. My heart's racing and my head's spinning so badly that I'm distracted from the awful stinging in my ass.

"Yes," she says, and pauses as we all look at her. "And isn't that awful..."

Candy, who's sitting next to me, reaches over and takes my hand, and smiles at me.

We're jolted from the silence in the room by a knock on the door. An aide stands in the doorway with my baby.

"She won't stop crying; I guess she wants her mommy." Miss Tina walks towards her and carefully cradles my baby in her arms before laying her gently in mine.

All the girls crowd around and the boys hang back a bit, but only because they can't get close enough because all the girls want to look at my baby.

"What's her name?" several kids ask.

I shrug. I don't know. A name seems so important and I'm not ready to make the decision, because the decision I make will be on my tongue until the day I die.

Miss Tina kneels at my feet.

"Now, remember what I said about recreating the environment she's known since the moment of conception. Yes, she may be hungry but look at her, her arms and legs are everywhere, they're thrashing about. She's never been uncontained before and it's frightening her. She needs to be wrapped in a papoose."

"You do it," I say, feeling awkward. I think I remember how to do it, but with all these kids watching me, I feel self-conscious.

Miss Tina takes my baby and lodges her on her shoulder with one hand while she spreads the blanket over my knees.

"Do it like this," she tells all the kids, girls and boys. "A baby needs to feel safe and secure. If it doesn't, it'll scream and get very distressed."

Miss Tina lays my baby on my lap and slowly and deliberately shows everyone how to wrap a baby so that it feels secure, and like before, it's magic. She stops screaming instantly.

"She's hungry," Miss Tina says. "Remember what I said about what happens when a baby experiences hunger? It gets distressed, so don't let your baby get this hungry; feed her and then her distress will vanish...she'll feel content."

"What, here?" I ask, feeling mortified. I can't get my breasts out in front of kids that I've only just met.

"Yes," Miss Tina says sternly. "This is what being grown up is all about. You're a mother now and your baby needs you. If you feel embarrassed...well, sweetheart, you're going to have to get over it."

She hands me a small towel and places it over my shoulder and the baby's head, and then helps me latch my baby onto my breast.

It's a bizarre moment. I'm surrounded by kids I've never met before, all staring at me feeding my baby, and all with gooey looks on their faces. I can feel her sucking on me hard, as if she's desperate, and it's not uncomfortable anymore, just weird. It's as if she's desperate to cling on to life, and the only way to do that is to draw something from me. I have an overwhelming urge to cry, yet I want to laugh, too, because it suddenly feels beautiful.

The boys drift away and I'm glad. I'm too young to be okay with having my breasts out of my bra in front of boys. I know that some girls at school don't care about showing their bodies to the boys, but this feels very different...there's nothing sexual about it at all, it almost feels sacred. Some of the girls leave, too, and I don't mind at all. Candy and a couple of other girls stay.

"You're so brave," one of them says. "I'm Mary, by the way."

"Doesn't it hurt to breast feed? My sisters have told me horrible things about it."

I shake my head.

"It was a bit uncomfortable at first, but that's because, when the milk comes in, it doesn't know when to stop. Once your baby starts to take what it needs from you, your body only makes the amount of milk your baby needs. It's pretty incredible."

I glance up and see Miss Tina smile at me. "You sound like an expert," she says, laughing.

I shift my baby over to my other breast, and Candy helps me move the towel over so that I can have some privacy.

When the baby is asleep with milk droplets rolling down her chin, Candy begs to hold her. I glance at Miss Tina to see if it's okay, and she nods. I carefully hand her over, but I feel a pang of anxiety as she leaves my arms.

Miss Tina says, "It's not a good idea to pass a new baby around. It distresses them, but she's full and sound asleep, so it won't matter right now. Normally I'd say that, although everyone wants to hold a new baby, you should say 'No,' because in those early days the baby needs to be with its mother and father, and no one else. A new baby is not a toy to be passed around."

Candy looks mortified, and my baby stirs. Can she feel Candy's anxiety? I don't know. How can something so small know so much? It's a miracle.

"Here, Hannah, take her back," Candy says, looking scared as she transfers her back into my arms. She looks scared that she'll drop her, and I'm scared too. She stirs and begins to wail.

I tighten the blanket around her and she stops and then sniffles as I put her on my shoulder and pat her butt to the same rhythm as my heartbeat. She's asleep immediately.

Miss Tina looks proud and I smile at her.

"It's time for bed," she says to me. "I know the others won't go to bed for ages yet, but you need your rest...it's part of being a new mother, so come on, let's go."

She gently takes the baby from me, and Candy helps me up. I'm so sore but I try not to show it because I don't want to have to explain what happens to your privates when you have a baby.

Candy gives me a hug, and she makes me feel like a million dollars.

I follow Miss Tina back to my room, shuffling like an old lady, tears about to fall as my ass hurts so badly.

She puts my baby down in her crib and runs my bath, and then she helps me to climb in so that I can soak my ripped butt in salt water. It's heaven, and I cry with relief, and for no reason that I can explain. She helps me climb back into bed when I'm dry, and I feel unbelievably tired. This is crazy...all I've done today is cuddle my baby, go to a group, and take a salt bath. Why am I so exhausted?

Miss Tina reminds me that my body and mind are adjusting to huge changes that make you feel exhausted...she's right because that's exactly how I feel.

I fall asleep in seconds, yet it seems that in no time an aide is shaking me so that I can feed my baby. I try to remember everything Miss Tina told me, and it seems to work. My baby feeds and I sniff her diaper to see if she needs changing, but she hasn't pooped so I don't change her. I raise her silently onto my shoulder and gently pat her back...only one little burp seeps out and I gently place her back into the crib beside my bed. I'm asleep in seconds and can't remember the aide taking my baby out of the room.

It seems as if it's only moments before they bring her back again for another feeding, and it's morning. I'm so bleary eyed. Why am I so exhausted?

Miss Tina breezes into the room.

"Good morning, Hannah. Did you sleep well?"

"Ugh, it's hard. The moment I fall asleep it seems as if I'm awakened again to feed my baby."

Miss Tina smiles.

"Yep, that's what it's like to start with. It'll get better, though, once she settles down. How's your butt feeling this morning?"

It seems so odd to be talking about such things at my age, when my friends have nothing else on their minds but eye shadow and the hottest bands.

"It hurts," I say, having no interest in eye shadow, and the last thing on my mind is sexy guys.

Going to the bathroom is agony, and I find that I cry at the drop of a hat. The bleeding has slowed down, and Miss Tina tells me that it's normal for it to turn a weird brown color.

"I'll run you another salty bath," she says, walking into the bathroom. "Y'know, some people don't believe that salty baths do anything to help, but if it works for you, then go with it."

It does help, it really does. I step into the water and lower myself down. Miss Tina asks me if I'm okay and then leaves me to waft the salty water around my body.

I don't know how long I've been soaking but the water starts to cool. I press the bell, and Miss Tina comes back to help me get out of the water. She puts a towel around me and places my slippers in front of me. I want to cry because I feel so frumpy, not at all like a teenager whose only concern is what to wear and who to be seen with. All I care about at the moment is the pain in my vagina...I can't even pee without it searing and burning.

Miss Tina tells me that I should rest this morning and spend time with my baby. The other kids have to go to group and then class, but she feels that my time should be spent with my baby, learning how to be a mother. It feels so weird...I should be at school learning algebra.

I nestle back into my pillows and Miss Tina puts my baby in my arms. She's asleep but snuffles, and her lips suck at nothing.

She's doesn't stir even when the cleaner comes in and makes a load of noise, so I edge out of bed and place her in her crib. Moments later Miss Tina pokes her head around the door and says, "You've got a visitor."

"Who?"

"Zak."

My face flushes and I feel instant panic.

"I can't see him."

She sits on the bed next to me and says gently, "Hannah, I know this is difficult, but it's not going to go away. Whether you like it or not, you have a child together, and he has a right to know his daughter."

I start crying and she pats my hand.

"Would you like me to sit in with you both?"

I nod miserably.

She comes back with Zak, looking as awkward as I feel. I know I'm blushing, and he looks pretty red, too.

He walks over to the crib and looks shocked.

Miss Tina tells him to sit down, and she pulls up another chair and sits opposite him. I stay on my bed and pull my knees up under my chin for protection. I don't want him to see how big my breasts are or that they leak everywhere.

I have no idea what to say. He has two vivid black eyes, and I feel ashamed that one of them came from my dad, and then I know what to say.

"I'm sorry about what my dad did to you."

He shrugs. "I deserved it."

Miss Tina shakes her head. "No, you don't deserve it; no one deserves to be beaten, no matter what they've done or not done."

We fall silent again. Miss Tina prompts him. "What d'you want to say to Hannah?"

"I want to say that I'm sorry for being so mean to you all the time. I was angry with you because your dad told my parents about the party. I'm sorry."

If I weren't so sore and trying to hide my heavy, leaking breasts, I'd have liked to fly at him and pummel his face into the floor. Does he think that by just saying "Sorry," it can wipe out all the pain he's caused me for nine months?

I grit my teeth and say nothing for a moment. I can feel tears prickling my eyes but I force myself to stop...I will not cry in front of him.

"It wasn't my fault that he told your parents; d'you think I wanted him to?" is all I can think to say.

He shrugs, "I thought you did. I thought you wanted to get me into trouble because you got into trouble with your dad."

"Why would you think that? Why would you think that I'd want to get you into trouble? I liked you."

He looks sheepish. "I dunno. I liked you, too."

"Well, you could have fooled me," I say, feeling bitter, as I think of the torment he's put me through. "You made my life miserable, day in and day out."

"I'm sorry, I'm sorry, all right! My life was hell, too, after your dad told my parents about the party. And in case you haven't noticed, they've made my life hell since your dad came over to our house again," he says, pointing to his black eyes.

"Well, that's not my fault either, is it?" I snap, hating him more than ever.

"What makes your dad think he's got the right to come to my house to get me into trouble? He's got no rights over me. Why couldn't he just be angry with you? He gave my parents the excuse they're always looking for to pick on me, and they've fed off it for months; and now he's done it again."

"Hold it, hold it," Miss Tina says. "Stop! This isn't going to help. Remember my favorite saying, 'There's no blame, only understanding.' Let's try and understand what's happened, okay?"

We look away from each other, the air electric between us.

At this moment I want to blame him for everything because I feel so angry with him, yet I also feel shy and embarrassed. I've just given birth to his baby, but I don't even know him. I really don't know what to do or say, and neither does he, because he stares at the floor.

Miss Tina looks at both of us and says, "It seems to me that your dad, Hannah, has some issues of his own and that he over-reacted on the night of the party. It seems as if he wanted to place the blame on someone else rather than on his own daughter."

"How? He was really mean to me, too," I say.

"Yes, he was, but it seems that his anger was diluted by unloading some of it onto Zak. I think that your dad loves you desperately, and he probably was scared that if he got too mad at you, you'd stop loving him. He sounds really vulnerable, Hannah; he needs you to love him, probably more than you need him to love you.

"It's likely that he didn't get enough love as a child and so he needs your mom, Jacky and you to make up for the love he didn't get. He seems determined to bring his children up differently and to have different values than those in his family, so seeing you drunk at Zak's party would have triggered some powerful emotions in him. He'd feel obliged to tell you off and ground you, and he was right to, yet he'd have felt wretched, fearing that you wouldn't love him anymore. It seems like he was projecting some of his anger and fear..."

I frown.

"...Yes, Hannah, fear...onto Zak and his parents in the hopes that his relationship with you wouldn't be ruined beyond repair."

"It is ruined, though," I say, though it suddenly makes sense.

"'There's no blame, only understanding.' Understand why he felt compelled to blame Zak and his parents, and then try to understand why Zak behaved the way he did to you. I know you both feel hurt at the moment, but there's no point in blaming each other. You just need to understand why it happened and how it all got to be so bad—that's all."

Zak shifts in his seat and I stare at the window, but Miss Tina carries on.

"It seems as if we have several issues here, the first being that you two have a daughter. Now, whether you're friends or not right now doesn't matter, because in the future you will have to develop some kind of relationship. At the very least you need to be civil to each other for the sake of your child. She needs two parents, a mother and a father, parents who can show each other respect. You will damage her if you both keep on fighting or arguing, so whatever has happened during the past nine months, you need to try and find a way through it so that you can start to build a new relationship for your daughter's sake."

I dare to glance at him with my face set; he's glaring at me, too.

"I think that you should express how you've both felt during the last nine months, and let's deal with it now so that it doesn't get in the way in the future. What d'you think?"

We both mutter, "Okay," begrudgingly.

"Hannah, what were you feeling after the party?"

"Embarrassed that I threw up everywhere, and ashamed that I let him have sex with me. I was a virgin..."

"You were?"

I stare hatefully at him.

"Yes, I was. Did you think I was a slut?"

"No. I really liked you. I...I...the boys at school say it's special to be a girl's first."

"It's supposed to be, but I was so drunk that I can't even remember it, and I hate that. Why did you do it when I was so drunk?"

Miss Tina looks at him, and he looks at the floor and mumbles, "I thought you wanted it, too, because you were laughing and grabbing at me."

I'm embarrassed; I can't remember doing that.

Miss Tina asks, "Zak, how did you feel after the party?"

"Worried about Hannah because her dad was mean—sorry, but he was. I thought she'd feel humiliated, the way he stormed into my house and took her out of there. I was also worried because she was so drunk, and I was scared that he'd hit her."

"My dad would never hit me," I say, defending his honor.

"Well, I didn't know that, did I? My dad hits me."

Miss Tina looks at him, and says, "Is that something you're used to, Zak?"

He looks at her as if she's stupid, given that he's got two fresh black eyes.

"Yeah, sure! My dad always uses his fists, especially after he's been drinking."

"Did your parents give you permission to have the party at their house?" she asks him.

"Nope."

"Then why did you have a party without permission, if your father has a volatile temper?"

"Dunno."

"Think! It's okay to talk here, we need to understand; there's no blame, only understanding."

"Because I wanted the kids at school to think I was cool," he says in a quiet voice, and I look at him differently. "I thought that I could have the party, clean up, and they'd never have known. And they wouldn't have, if your dad hadn't come over and told them."

"I'm sorry, but it's not my fault," I say.

"Zak, it really isn't Hannah's fault that her

father behaved the way he did, not nine months ago or when he found out about the baby. You have to accept some responsibility for having the party at your house without your parents' permission, especially knowing that they would be mad. But having said that, it's not your responsibility that they were violent towards you, and it's not right that they are. You need to know that I am going to be reporting them."

"No! Don't! You'll make it ten times worse for me. Hell, I knew I shouldn't have come."

He stands up and starts to head for the door.

Miss Tina gets up, too. "Zak, stop! Sit down! Your parents may have been angry or disappointed in you, but that doesn't give them the right to beat you; it's against the law, it's abusive, and it has to stop. I don't care what you've done or what you haven't done, it's not right for them to beat you, and they have to stop."

He turns back towards her and there are tears in his eyes. I feel bad for hating him. No matter what I think of my dad at the moment, I know that he's a good dad and has never beaten us. I can't imagine what it must be like to be subjected to a father who beats you just because you've made him mad.

"Sit down and let's talk. None of this is going to go away, so we have to talk it through."

He sits back down and the baby starts to cry.

Miss Tina goes to her crib and picks her up,

patting her back and crooning into the creases of her neck, and I know that she's trying to recreate the same environment that my baby knew when she was inside me. She stops crying immediately. Miss Tina looks at me, and I know what she's asking. I give her a bleak smile, and she hands the baby to Zak.

His anger has crumpled and a weird look of wonder has slid onto his face. I resist the urge to laugh.

He clears his throat like there's something stuck in it, and he says, "Man, she's beautiful; she looks like you."

"Thanks."

"You're welcome."

Miss Tina sits back down and she's smiling.

Zak suddenly looks different. His face is softer, his anger's gone, and I feel the tension in my jaw disappear. We all just stare at the baby.

"What're you going to call her?" Zak asks, and they both look at me.

"I don't know. I've been thinking about it and I want her name to mean something. I can remember the first time you came to our school, Miss Tina, and talked about drinking alcohol and peer pressure. I thought, 'I wish she'd come to the school on the Friday, the day before the party; then I would never have gotten drunk and *it* would never have happened.' But when I look into my baby's eyes and she stares at me, I feel so much love for her that I can't imagine ever living without her, so that I'm glad you came to teach us on the Monday, after the party. So I want to call her 'Monday.'"

I look at them both. Miss Tina's smiling and Zak says, "Monday?" and then he says it several times, as if he's trying to make it fit his tongue. Then he looks at me and says, "I like it." He pauses and holds my gaze.

"Hannah, I'm glad Miss Tina taught you on the Monday and not the Friday, and I really *am* sorry for being such a jerk."

# Chapter Ten

It's awkward when he leaves because something has changed between us, although I don't really know what it is. He gives Monday a kiss on her forehead before handing her back to Miss Tina, and then he stands in the doorway staring at me.

"I'm sorry, Hannah, I really am. I know you probably won't think I'm for real, or trust me, but can I come to see you both again? Please?"

I nod, feeling strange, and then he's gone.

Miss Tina hands Monday to me as she needs to be fed, and while the baby latches onto me, Miss Tina sits and talks.

"Well, that went well, don't you think? I know he hurt you, Hannah, but I think he's been hurt himself." I know she sees me flinch. "It's not a competition to see who's been hurt the most, but we need to recognize that he *has* been hurt, too.

I'm not joking when I say that I'm going to report his parents for their abuse of him. He doesn't need to put up with that...no child does."

I'm silent for a while because it feels strange to think thoughts about Zak that aren't hateful.

"At least my dad doesn't beat me," is all I can think of to say.

"No, but abuse comes in many forms. Although physical abuse is the most obvious, there can be emotional abuse as well. Manipulating someone by withdrawing love or by emotional blackmail are also forms of abuse, so while I'm glad that your dad doesn't beat you, I'm still as concerned about you as I am about Zak."

I'm torn between wanting to stand up for my dad and relief that someone is standing up for me.

"I love the name 'Monday,'" Miss Tina says, "and it made me feel very special when you told us the reasons for her name."

"I've thought about it so much over the past nine months. At first I cursed that you hadn't taught us on the Friday, because if you had, I know that I wouldn't have done what I did, and I wouldn't have gotten pregnant..."

I fall silent for a moment as thoughts engulf me. If I had it all to do again, I wouldn't wish to have a baby, to drop out of school, to be excluded from the running and the trampoline teams, to be the hot gossip at school, and to have no certainty in my future anymore. I can't be certain that I'll ever go to college, or that I'll ever have a career, money and choices like Linda and all my friends at school will have...those days have gone for me.

I don't know what my future is going to hold. I want to finish school, but from now on it's not a certainty. It'll only happen if grown-ups help me, and that means that they'll have to put their lives on hold so that I can move forward as I was supposed to...the same as my peers.

Looking at Monday snuggling into my breast and coiling her finger around mine, I know that my future will revolve around her. It's completely changed from how it was nine months ago, with my parents' plans for me to follow Jacky to college; I know that's not going to happen right now. I know that I'm not going to be able to hang out the same as my friends, or go out in the evenings, or even date, because I've got a baby to take care of, and I have to put her first. I know that even if I am able to finish school, I can never go away to college and have all the fun that Mom and Dad tell us they had once they were away from their parents' rules.

I look at Monday; Zak thinks she looks like me, and he said she was beautiful. Does that mean that he thinks I'm beautiful, too?

I feel so confused that I don't even dare to allow myself to think about him, yet I know I'm going to have to at some point. I think that Monday looks like my dad, heaven help her, but I swear she does, and it's a strange feeling.

Miss Tina coughs, jolting me from my thoughts.

"But y'know, Miss Tina, I can't be sorry that you taught us on the Monday instead of the Friday because I can't imagine not having my baby with me now that she's here. That's why I want to call her Monday; it means something to me."

She smiles at me; it's a smile that touches somewhere deep inside me, somewhere that belongs to Miss Tina, a place where I know I'm accepted for who I am, a place where there's no blame.

"Well, she means something to me, as you do too," she says.

After lunch I go to the Group Room and join the other kids. They all want to know where Monday is...she's sleeping, and an aide is watching her.

Miss Tina waits until everyone is quiet and then looks at me.

"We share the things that happen to us here so everyone can learn from each other's experiences, okay?"

I nod, wondering what she's going to say.

"This morning Hannah's baby's father came to see her, and he said something that really made me think."

I look at her, my face feeling red, and I wonder which bit of everything he said had caught her attention.

She looks around the room and explains what happened this morning. "After he apologized for the way he'd treated her for nine months, he said, 'I know you probably won't think I'm for real, or trust me, but can I come to see you both again?' I thought that was a mature thing to say because he recognized that after his awful behavior towards Hannah, she would be unlikely to trust him. So, today we're going to look at trust—what it is, how it's gained, how it's broken and how to get it back once it's gone. Because even though we may apologize for something we've done wrong, and be forgiven, it doesn't automatically mean that there will be trust in the relationship anymore."

She walks to the flipchart and writes at the top of four pages, "What is trust?" and "How is trust gained?" Then she writes, "How is trust broken?" and "How can you get trust back once it's gone?" Then she sits down.

"Mary, will you come and write everything down under these headings, please?"

Mary gives us a little bow as she stands in front of the flipchart.

Miss Tina grins at her, and says, "Right, let's start at the beginning. What is trust? Just call out what you think it is; there are no right or wrong answers."

Mike is the first to speak. "It's something you feel, something that makes you feel safe."

Miss Tina says, "Say more."

"I think it's when you believe someone is telling the truth and will do what they say they are going to do."

Miss Tina nods.

Candy says, "I think it could be when you expect a person to behave a certain way and they always do."

"That's called 'consistency,'" Miss Tina says.

I venture to speak out.

"I think trust is when you know that no matter what you say or do, you'll be accepted."

Miss Tina looks at me for a moment while the room goes quiet, and Mary scribbles furiously, trying to keep up with our suggestions of what trust really is.

"It's when a person is always there and never lets you down," a kid says.

"It's when they don't change their minds."

"It's when someone is always there for you."

"Hey, hold on, I'm running out of paper," Mary says laughing.

Miss Tina stands up and walks over to the flip-chart and points to the first thing Mary wrote.

"All these things describe trust really well, but I think I like what Mike said first of all, 'It's something you feel, something that makes you feel safe.' All the other examples you've called out come down to these two things. If people let you down, you feel bad and you don't feel safe."

She sticks the paper on the wall and then points to the second statement, "How is trust gained?"

"So, how *is* trust gained?" she asks.

"Well, that's easy," Mike says. "Look at what Mary's written. Trust can be gained when all those things are there."

"Explain, please," Miss Tina says, but I already know what he means.

"Well, it's obvious. Trust can be gained when you believe someone is telling you the truth, and they do what they say they're going to do, and when they keep their promises. You have trust in people when they behave in the way you expect them to behave, and when they are consistent. Then you can feel trust in other people when you're accepted, even though your attitudes may be different than theirs."

He looks a little irritated, as if this is too easy.

"You can gain trust when people never let you down, or change their minds, and when they are always there for you."

Miss Tina says, "So when you feel trust, it feels good and you feel safe?"

We nod.

She asks, "How is trust broken?"

Everyone seems to have something to say. The room is full of kids talking over each other.

"When someone promises you something and

then lets you down."

"When others withhold things from you and won't tell you what they're thinking."

"When people are being secretive; my boyfriend was like that and he was seeing someone else."

"When people won't tell you what they're feeling."

"When people say one thing but do another, and the look on their face doesn't match their tone of voice."

"When somebody lies to you."

"Yes," Miss Tina says, "As you can see there are plenty of ways to lose trust in people. Losing trust makes you feel bad, and also makes you feel unsafe. Let's think about it in another way: Why do people lie? Everyone lies at some time; why?"

"Because they're scared they'll be judged."

"Because they think they're not good enough."

"Because they're scared of the consequences of telling the truth."

"Because they don't trust another person enough to tell them the truth."

Mary stands in front of the flipchart, scribbling down our answers.

"Oh, my," Miss Tina says, "look at how much you've all covered. Okay...let's take a moment to think about how some of you have lost your family's trust, why you felt that you had to lie, and how you can get that trust back again."

I feel very hot and uncomfortable, and a lot of kids shift in their seats.

It's obvious to me how I lost my parents' trust...I behaved in the way they hate. I got drunk and then got pregnant without being married. I behaved exactly like their families, after they'd tried so hard to be different from them, and had raised Jacky and me to be different so that they'd be proud of us.

Why did I lie to them? I lied because I was terrified, and because I couldn't bear to witness my dad's disappointment in me. I've never felt good enough for him or Mom, and never as good as Jacky. I lied because I didn't trust them to accept me as being different from Jacky. I lied because I didn't believe that they would help me without making me feel like dirt, as if I was worthless. And then I lied because I couldn't see any way back from all the lies I'd already told, and lies I'd committed by omission...by doing things I shouldn't have or by not doing what I should have.

How can I get trust back again? That feels impossible. I know I've done wrong, but I feel that my parents have lied to me, too. They haven't been "real" about why they were so desperate to be different from their families. They've lied by omission. They haven't been truly honest about their love for Jacky and me; their love feels conditional. It feels like they'll only love us if we "perform" for them so that they can boast about our successes. I can't see my dad changing the way he feels about his family or allowing Jacky and me to be ourselves. He wants to be able to brag about us, and that means we have to be the kind of people he wants us to be. I don't think we'll ever trust each other again because I don't think trust was ever really there in the first place.

I sit still and don't say anything when the other kids shout out their answers. Mary tears off another page from the flipchart, and Miss Tina pins it to the wall. It's all too raw for me, and I feel like crying.

Miss Tina notices my silence and hones in on me.

"Hannah, what're your thoughts?"

I wish the floor would open into a deep chasm and let me fall, for all the thoughts that are making my head spin cascade out of me, and I can't stop myself from sobbing.

All the kids are quiet until I stop crying.

"What is it that you want, Hannah?" Miss Tina asks.

Candy hands me a box of tissues, and I think for a moment before speaking, trying to gain control of myself.

"I want my dad to accept me as I am, and I want him to realize that I'm not Jacky. I feel so bad that I lied to him and Mom for nine months, and I know that I'll never be able to apologize enough to make it right. Mom seems to be able to forgive me...she wants me to come home and says that she'll help me with Monday, but I want my dad to accept the reasons why I couldn't tell him that I was in trouble and needed his help."

I know I'm only a kid and parents talk all the time about being able to trust their children, but what about kids being able to trust their parents?

"Trust is a delicate thing," Miss Tina says, "and there's little doubt that the trust between you and your dad has been broken, and you will both have to work on trying to repair it. Trust works both ways...it isn't one-sided."

I look at her, feeling heard, but hopeless.

"I don't know how to make my dad trust me, and I don't know how to trust him," I say.

Miss Tina thinks for a moment and then says, "If we understand that trust is the 'glue' that keeps us all connected to each other, then without it we're isolated and alone. It's a two-way process and it can only remain strong if we're honest with each other. Honesty is what will repair trust that's broken."

I blow my nose but it runs again almost immediately, and my eyes are brimming with tears. I feel awful and have an overwhelming urge to go and cuddle Monday...I love her so much and I pray that she'll never feel what I'm feeling right now. I'm determined that, even though I'm only a kid, I'm going to make sure that she and I are honest with each other, so that we can trust each other. I want her to feel good and to feel safe. No matter who she is and turns out to be, I promise I'll accept her for who she is.

I sit in my chair and ignore my sore butt, for my heart hurts more. I long for group to be over, because I want my baby so badly that I fear I'm going to start crying all over again.

Miss Tina beams at us. "You kids are awesome." She points to the flipchart pages stuck around the room. "Look at everything you've covered today. Even though it's caused you pain to think about these things, you did it anyway."

I feel a watery smile spread across my face as we all look at each other. As kids smile at me, I drift off to a place where I silently determine that I'm going to talk to my dad honestly, even if he doesn't like what I'm saying...I've got nothing to lose. I don't think I've got any chance of regaining his trust, or me trusting him again, until we can be honest with each other. I feel scared but resigned. This is how it's going to have to be. This is what I want Monday to do with me when she's my age, if we ever lose the trust between us.

"Remember, trust is a two-way process; both people in a relationship have to be honest. When trust is broken, you have to build bridges if you want to regain that trust, and you build bridges by being honest.

"I have a little story to help you think about everything we've talked about."

She grins at us and starts reading.

• • • •

*Far, far away in the land that bobbed in and out of view depending upon the sea mist, a tribe of people lived among the hills. There were so many steep hills and deep valleys that the people felt as if they were living on a colony of giant anthills.*

*The people were a covetous tribe, always wanting what their neighbors had. They were consumed by making sure that their neighbors didn't have more than they had, and they always tried to outdo each other. Every family built their house on top of a hill and made them as grand as they could. Although they waved at their neighbors each morning as the sun rose and again as they sat beneath their ornate porches, watching the sun slip below the hilly horizon as night fell, envy filled their hearts.*

*The children had fun together playing in the deep valleys between the hills, yet they knew anxiety in their hearts. Every night as the children ate supper, they listened to their parents berate their neighbors, and they warned the children not to reveal what each family had. They taught their children how to hide their feelings for fear of being judged, and they taught them how to be secretive so that others would not know how much their families were worth. As they taught their children* to tell lies, no one had any trust in anyone, and they hid the truth in their hearts.

On the highest hill grew a beautiful weeping willow tree that reached into the heavens. It was a tree like no other, a sacred tree. Legend told the people that the Gods of the Trees lived within that great tree, but no one had ever seen them or knew for sure that they were there. But they _were_ there, and the gods watched in dismay as their people told lies and had no trust in themselves or each other.

One night a small child lay shivering in his bed, listening to a storm raging outside and the trees breaking in the deep valleys below him, when he heard the Gods of the Trees' cries on the wind.

"Help us before we perish. A deadly fungus is about to creep up the highest hill where our sacred weeping willow tree reaches up to the heavens. You must make a ring of fire around the bottom of our hill to kill the deadly fungus so that the sacred weeping willow tree will be saved. Hurry, there's no time to lose."

The little boy thought he was dreaming, but he heard the gods' cries again and ran to wake up his father.

"Go back to sleep," his father said. "It's just a dream; it's just the storm. There's no such thing as a sacred weeping willow tree, and certainly no gods are living in it."

He scoffed and laughed, but the little boy stood firm and trusted in the small voice within him that told him he was right.

"We have to go, now!" he said. "I trust what I heard. We must hurry. We have to save the sacred weeping willow tree on the highest hill; it's important," and not waiting for his father, he ran to the door and hurried out into the storm.

He ran down into the deep valleys where he played with his friends every day, and he made his way towards the highest hill. After a while, his father caught up with him. His father looked at his son and saw faith and trust in his face. Although he couldn't hear the gods' cries, his mistrust wavered when he saw how urgent his son was, so he trusted that his son had, indeed, heard the gods' cries.

"A deadly fungus is about to creep up the highest hill where the sacred weeping willow tree reaches up to the heavens," the little boy said with panic in his voice. "We have to make a ring of fire around the bottom of the hill to kill the deadly fungus, so that the sacred weeping willow tree will be saved."

They were soaked to the skin but worked for hours gathering wood, and as lightning flashed around them and trees were burned to a cinder and crashed to the valley floor, they worked on. They stacked a massive bonfire in a ring around the bottom of the highest hill, beneath the sacred *weeping willow tree.*

*The child's father lit the fire, and they watched it burn brightly around the hill as the storm abated. As the sun peeped over the horizon bringing a new day, the flames shot into the dawn: orange, red, yellow, green and purple, a fiery dance of triumph that burned and ebbed to a glow around the highest hill, where the sacred weeping willow tree remained unscathed.*

*The Gods of the Trees looked upon the small boy who had trust in his heart—the small boy who had saved their sacred tree—and they gave him a gift, one to share with all the people. They gave him a seed from the sacred weeping willow tree for each family to grow on top of their hill outside their homes. The seed was to teach them that the small boy had trusted the gods' cries for help, and his father had trusted that the boy had not been lying.*

*Each family planted their seed right outside their homes and watered it daily, anxious for their tree to grow faster and be bigger than their neighbors'. Only the little boy and his father remembered why the Gods of the Trees had given them the gift, and even though they tried to tell their neighbors of their trees' meaning, they refused to listen. All they cared about was having the tallest tree with the most leaves, so that they could boast that theirs was the best.*

*Years later the weeping willow trees stood proud and tall, offering shade in the midday sun and peace beneath its hanging branches. But still the people did not value the gift that the Gods of the Trees had given them, and they were totally unconcerned about why the gift had been given. They did not care that the small boy, who had grown into a strong man, had trusted the gods' cries and that his father had trusted that his son had not been lying to him.*

*The people continued to judge each other, to brag that their tree was better than their neighbors'. They were unable to be honest or truthful for fear of being judged, and they encouraged their children to lie, lest their true thoughts and fears would be discovered. They each lived in fear that their neighbors would find out that they had no more or no less than each other; and they didn't know how to live with that knowledge.*

*The Gods of the Trees had given their gift but, unbeknownst to the people, the weeping willow trees wept when in the presence of those who lied. With each lie that was uttered, the trees wept, and over time the deep valleys where the children played became flooded.*

*As the people failed to see the truth in their hearts and were afraid to question themselves to find out who they really were, lies slipped from their tongues in an attempt to hide their fear. Each* person feared that they were not as good as their neighbors and that someone would find out. Not one person, except the small boy who had grown into a strong man, and his father, knew the truth... that each person had no need to lie or to hide who they really were, for all were equally valuable and unique.

The children were unable to play with their friends as the deep valleys were flooded and they had no way to reach each other. Each family was isolated on their hilltop, and fearing the rising water, they worked on their homes to make them impenetrable.

They shouted across the rising water at their neighbors, unwilling to tell the truth that they were afraid and didn't know what to do. They boasted about how well they were doing and that everything was fine. But as they uttered each lie, the weeping willow trees shed more tears, and the water rose until it lapped around their grand houses on the top of each hill.

The people were terrified, fearing that they'd all drown. The children longed for each other, to play together in the deep valleys, and to share the truths in their hearts. But they were isolated on top of their hills, separated by the lies that were told, and the rising flood of tears. They knew pain in their hearts. The adults didn't know what to do and feared that their tribe would be lost forever.

One night the Gods of the Trees spoke to the young man in his dreams telling him what to do to save the people. Later that day the young man and his father sat beneath their weeping willow tree, the peace beneath its hanging branches gone, and spoke to each other as no other person in that land of hills could. They spoke with honesty in their hearts, and neither lied, for they had no fear of being judged by each other.

The young man told his father, "The Gods of the Trees gave us a gift, part of the sacred weeping willow that reaches up into the heavens, because you and I trusted each other and didn't tell lies. Everyone seems to be afraid that if they stop telling lies and show who they really are, they'll be judged by others. Everyone lives a lie for fear of being judged. No one is able to be honest with themselves and others, and no one trusts anyone. This isn't how the gods want us to live. We shall all perish if our people don't learn how to be truthful, for without honesty there can be no trust. We have to build bridges to reach our neighbors and show them how to be honest."

He looked out towards the horizon, and there were many hilltops with grand houses and weeping willow trees separated from each other by a sea of tears. Each family and each person was an island, alone and isolated, separated because they had no trust in each other.

The young man looked up at the weeping willow tree above him as the water crept over his shoes, soaking his feet.

He said, "The Gods of the Trees gave us this gift to help our people learn about trust, but they have not learned. They have used this gift to brag that theirs is better than their neighbors', and they have tried to outdo each other for fear of being judged as inferior.

"We have to use the branches to build a bridge to reach our neighbors, so that we can teach them about honesty and trust."

The old man nodded, trusting his son completely. They spent the whole evening and night chopping branches from their weeping willow tree and built a bridge that would allow them to reach one of their neighbors. But when the morning came, they saw that the bridge wasn't long enough.

They shouted to their neighbor, begging them to use the wood from their weeping willow tree so that they could build a bridge that would meet theirs half way across the flooded valley.

They refused at first because they didn't want to ruin their beautiful tree, for then their neighbors would have something they didn't have and would look down on them. They were also afraid as they didn't want anyone coming too close to them. But when they saw how high the water had risen and feared that they might drown, they agreed to build *a bridge using some of the wood from their fine weeping willow tree.*

*They worked all day, and as the evening came, they edged gingerly across their half of the bridge and fastened it securely to that of the young man and his father.*

*The neighbors were so relieved to no longer be alone that they cooked a fine supper and talked around the table.*

*Their children glanced at each other, longing to play as they had done in the deep valleys before the weeping willow trees had wept.*

*"Can we build a bridge to our other neighbors?" they begged. "We miss our friends."*

*Their parents glanced anxiously at each other. Building bridges and meeting people halfway meant allowing others to see what they had...to see the real them. They wouldn't be able to pretend to be better than anyone else anymore. They'd have to stop lying and be honest.*

*They were about to say "No" when the young man and his father said, "It's the only thing we can do to save our people. We have to build bridges and to get to know each other properly so that we don't have to lie anymore, and we'll be able to trust each other."*

*The neighbors looked shocked, but the young man told them what the Gods of the Trees had said in his dreams. He told them of the seed they'd been* given, a gift that was supposed to teach the people about trust and honesty.

"It seems that our people have not understood what the gift means. They have taken the gift but have not learned from it; instead they have been in competition with each other and have been boastful. They have not learned that the seed was a gift to the people to teach them about trust. Our people have continued to lie for fear of being judged, and as each lie was uttered, the weeping willow trees have wept, flooding our beautiful deep valleys. Trust me, the only way to stop the weeping willow trees from weeping is to be honest and stop lying."

The children cried.

"I hate having to tell lies. Why can't I tell the truth?" one of the children asked his father. "Does it matter that we don't really have lots of gold and fine silk curtains? My friends don't care...I don't care. I just want to play with my friends again. I feel as if I'm in a prison, stuck on top of this hilltop with nowhere to go and no one to play with. Please, can we use our weeping willow tree to build bridges so that we can reach our other neighbors and play with our friends?"

His children continued to cry.

"Why can't I tell my friends what I'm feeling?" his eldest daughter asked. "I have no one to talk to; no one is honest. I hate lying because when I do, no one trusts me."

Silence hung in the air, except for the sound of the rising water lapping around their grand house on top of the hill.

The children nodded, all eager to speak first.

"I hate it when you lie about us having fine silk curtains when they're made of cotton," the eldest girl said.

"I hate it when you lie about our weeping willow tree, saying it was given to us because we're better than our neighbors," the eldest boy said.

"I feel embarrassed when you look down on my friends," a younger child said honestly.

"I feel hurt when I know you're lying to me," the youngest child said.

The young man and his father saw shock on their neighbors' faces as their children spoke the truth for the first time.

"Being honest is the only way we can really know each other," the young man said, "and when people are honest, you can trust them. If people lie there can be no honesty, and without honesty there can be no trust."

As he spoke, silence hovered in the room. He didn't know whether it was because the children's parents were afraid, shocked at their children's honesty, or uncomfortable at having someone in their home where their true selves were laid bare to be seen as they really were.

*The eldest child spoke, breaking the silence. "I can't hear the water lapping around the house," he said.*

*They all held their breaths, trying to be quiet, and he was right—the sound of water lapping around the grand house on the hilltop had gone.*

*They all rushed to the door and saw that the water had receded ten feet.*

*The young man spoke.*

*"This is what the Gods of the Trees told me would happen. If we're honest with each other and stop telling lies, then we can trust each other; we'll be accepted by each other, and no one will be judged by another. If we use our weeping willow trees, the gift the gods gave us to teach us about trust, to build bridges and connect with our neighbors, we'll never be alone or isolated again. We should not be afraid, for we are all different and yet we all belong to the same tribe; every one of us is part of it and we are equally valuable in our own way. Do not be afraid to be honest, for it is the only way we can trust in each other."*

*As he spoke, the water receded even more and the weeping willow trees stopped weeping.*

*Over the next few days the young man, his father and their neighbors, who were now excited and eager to be honest about themselves, worked from dawn to dusk to build bridges to reach their people. As they helped everyone to understand* the gift the Gods of the Trees had given them, the people began to relax. They chopped their weeping willow trees down and used the wood to build bridges to reach out to each other.

Every day the waters receded as the people opened their hearts and spoke honestly about themselves and their feelings, and as the water finally soaked into the valley floor, their children rejoiced. They ran down into the deep valleys and played as they had never played before. They shared their feelings, laughed with each other, and didn't care whose house was the grandest.

The children showed their parents how to be real, to be honest, and to live in a world where lies had no place, and gradually the people who lived in the land of steep hills and deep valleys learned how to trust each other. They were never alone again and no one judged anyone else; each person, although different, was as valuable as his neighbor.

The children played happily, showing their feelings honestly.

The young man and his father smiled, relieved that at last their people understood the gift they'd been given by the Gods of the Trees.

The gods were content and watched as the people learned how to trust each other, to break down the barriers they'd built around themselves for fear of being judged. They smiled and rested in *their sacred weeping willow tree that reached up to the heavens from the highest hilltop.*

# Chapter Eleven

Miss Tina smiles at us all and puts the papers down.

"So, Hannah, how does this story apply to your situation?"

"Uh, the people tried to outdo each other and thought they were better than each other. That's like my parents, who think they're better than their families."

"My parents are like that, too," Mike says.

"The only thing the people were concerned about was how many material things they had, and they wanted others to be jealous of them." I think for a moment. "I don't think my parents are like that, though. They don't really care about material things, but they do think their values are better than other people's...well, their families'."

It dawns on me that that's not actually true.

"Actually they don't only feel that way about their families; they feel that way about Zak and his family, and about Linda, too."

I remember what Zak said. "What gave my dad the right to go to his house and tell his parents that they weren't being good parents?" I remember Dad saying mean things about Linda and her "sort," too.

What if my family, Zak's and Linda's were on top of one of the hills, each trying to hide what was going on inside our homes? Zak's parents don't hide what's going on in their home very well...his bruises tell everyone. I think the clues to what goes on in Linda's home are that she believes she has to lie to get what she wants, and then her brother uses violence to get what he wants. I shiver, as the thought of my pink panties flashes into my head. I don't think anyone would have been able to guess what happened in our house, well, not until I suddenly gave birth, that is. I suppose I'm like one of the little kids in the story. I've learned to lie, to hide who I really am, so that my parents feel safe.

I say everything I'm thinking to the group, except the bit about my pink panties, and Miss Tina nods.

"How d'you think the children in the story felt?" she asks.

Mary says, "Even though they played together, I think they felt bad because they knew all the mean things their parents had said about each kid's family. It would be hard to be really close friends with someone when you knew that your parents, who you loved, didn't like your friend; you'd feel torn in two."

"That's how I felt about my friend Linda," I say. "I hated the way my dad said awful things about her...she's a good person. I couldn't tell her the things he said because she'd be hurt, so I felt as if I was holding out on her and couldn't be really honest with her. It affected our friendship. Well, in the end...in the end I couldn't be honest with her about anything..."

The kids look at me.

"I felt alone, as if I were pretending to be friends. I wasn't being real."

Miss Tina nods, listening to us.

"What d'you think about the small boy and his father?" she asks.

"I think," Mike says, "that the kid was strong. Perhaps little kids trust more than older kids. I think that he forced his father to have faith in him."

"Perhaps little kids have more faith than older kids," Candy says.

"My dad says that the older you get, the more cynical you get," Mary says.

Miss Tina smiles.

"I think it shows that adults can learn a lot from their children," I say, silently praying that my dad will learn something from me.

The kids say, "Yeah."

"What d'you think about how the people treated the gift the Gods of the Trees had given them?" Miss Tina asks.

Mary speaks out. "They didn't seem to be able to think about anything other than how other people saw their weeping willow trees...they missed the point completely."

My head's spinning. "That's like my dad, missing the point completely."

"How?" Miss Tina asks, forcing me to think.

"Well, he was upset about what everyone would think of our family, the way things looked on the outside. He was really upset that I'd lied to him, and 'brought shame upon the family,' so he didn't ask himself why I felt that I had to lie to him...and that's the point, isn't it?"

Candy nods, like she agrees.

"And he was so concerned with what the neighbors would say, and what his family would say, that he couldn't see there was no trust between us. Isn't that the same as the people in the story missing the point of the gift the gods had given them?"

"Very good," Miss Tina says. "You're thinking, that's good. That's what stories are for...to make you think."

"D'you know what I think?" Mary says, frowning. "I think that each family was scared."

"Say more," Miss Tina says.

"Of course they'd be scared as the water rose and they thought they'd drown, but they were scared before the water came."

Miss Tina beams at her, as if she's just found a treasure.

"They were scared that other people would judge them, so they isolated themselves, believing that if they hid their true selves, they'd be safe. But they weren't because, when everyone hid their true selves, nobody trusted anyone, and then they felt more isolated and more scared."

"Well done, Mary. So, Hannah, think about what Mary's just said. D'you think that your parents were scared in some way?"

I don't know what to say...I've never thought of them being scared; mean, yes, snobby, yes, but not scared.

"What would they be scared of?" I ask, shrugging.

"Think about it, girl," Mary says. "C'mon."

"Hmmm..."

Candy comes to my rescue.

"Perhaps they were scared that other people would judge them and say that they hadn't been good parents." I look at her and feel goosebumps prickle my skin. "You said that they were desperate to be different than their own parents, so maybe they were scared that people would say they were the *same* as their parents."

"Yes," Miss Tina nods. "What other reasons could make them feel scared?"

My brain is chugging like a heavy train going up hill. "Well, perhaps they were scared because they didn't really know how to be parents." I know I'm scared to be a mother because I don't know what I'm doing.

"That's a good point," Miss Tina says. "After all, their own parents hadn't been good role models."

Mike looks at me and speaks out. "If your parents have tried to distance themselves from their families for years and have been mean about them, perhaps they're scared that their families would retaliate and laugh at them."

I think Mike's right.

"Yes, Dad's been so mean about his and Mom's families, and now that I've 'brought shame' upon our family, they'll rip him to pieces," I say, feeling terrible.

The kids are nodding.

"That would be pretty scary," Miss Tina says. "I think that your parents, particularly your dad, must be terrified at this moment. They must have realized that they have failed in some way, even though they've been really good parents in other ways. They will have to face themselves, they will have to be honest about themselves and everything they've done, or haven't done, and that's scary...very."

I feel sick. I hate to think of my parents being scared, and I hate to think that I have "brought shame" on them, and their families will laugh at them because of me.

I say how I'm feeling and Miss Tina says, "It is not your fault that your parents isolated themselves from their families. You can have different values without believing that you're better than other people, and without putting others down. The reason they'll have to cope with their families' judgment of them is because *they* made it that way, not you."

She looks at me and says, "Hannah, everyone's journey through life is their own, and the lessons they learn are their own. I think that your parents will move along their journey through life in leaps and bounds if they examine the reasons why you couldn't tell them something as important as being pregnant. If they are able to understand the reasons you lied for nine months, they'll be like the people in the story who learned the real meaning of the gift the gods had given them...they will finally 'get the point.'"

I hope so.

"What can I do?" I say, feeling helpless. "I don't know what to do."

"What did the people in the story do?"

"They built bridges, and were honest with each other," I say.

Miss Tina nods. "Yes, and that's what you have to do. Reach out to him, even if you're scared that he's going to be mean...remember, he's probably scared. Then, be honest, because it's only through being honest that trust can grow."

I nod. I *am* scared, but I'm going to be honest with my dad. I know that he's always wanted the best for us, even if one of the reasons was because he needed to brag to his family that he was better than they were, but he's given Jacky and me a good life.

I'm so relieved when group is finally finished because I feel really tired. I don't know if it's because group was so tough today, but all I want to do is flop into bed. Candy comes back with me from the Group Room, and Monday's crib is already there. I have an overwhelming urge to cry. What *is* happening to me? I've never felt so volatile, not even through the past nine months when my life was hell. What's happening to me?

Candy helps me into bed, as my ass smarts badly, and sits beside me, staring at Monday in her crib. She really is content. She's wrapped like an Indian papoose with her little fingers right in front of her mouth, and every so often she snuffles and sucks on them until she drifts off to sleep again. She looks as if she doesn't have anything to worry about...she's lucky.

All sorts of feelings flood over me at once and

my eyes brim with tears.

"What's wrong?" Candy asks.

I shrug, feeling stupid.

"C'mon," she smiles. "Be honest."

I blow my nose.

"I'm just being silly. I know I've lied really badly and let my parents down, but I feel let down by them, too."

I shrug.

"I just don't know how to build bridges with my dad; Mom's okay, but Dad is just so rigid in the way he thinks. I'm determined to be honest when I speak to him, but I don't know if he can be with me. What do I do then? I'm scared. If he can't be honest with me and accept me for who I am, then what am I going to do? I don't think I can face his disappointment in me, and live with his 'silent treatment' everyday. But I don't really have a choice because I can only keep Monday if I live at home."

Tears fall down my face as the thought of not being able to keep Monday horrifies me.

Candy hugs me and tells me that it'll all be okay, and I just have to keep trying to be honest with my dad, even if he can't be with me.

"Hopefully he'll learn one day," she says, "like the people isolated on top of the hills, pretending to be something they weren't, because they were scared. Just keep being honest and keep trying, then maybe one day, if you're in his face all the time," she grins, "he'll have to accept you for who you are...even if he doesn't like it."

She makes me laugh, and I blow my nose. She sets me straight and I feel stronger. Yes, I'm going to be "in his face all the time" with my honesty, and even if I haven't turned out like he wanted me to, perhaps he'll accept who I really am.

She hugs me again and plants a kiss on my cheek, saying she'll see me tomorrow, and I feel loved. I know how the people in Miss Tina's story felt when the weeping willow trees' tears soaked into the ground and the kids were able to play together again.

I feel soothed and pick Monday up. I get back into bed carefully and hold her close to me. She snuffles and sleeps on my chest. I whisper into her ear and pat her butt to the same rhythm of my heartbeat, shutting out thoughts of my dad.

I feel peaceful, but not for long. Miss Tina pokes her head around the door and says, "Hannah, you've got a visitor."

I freeze as my dad stands in the doorway.

He doesn't seem to know where to look. He doesn't meet my eye and I feel panicked. Monday wakes up immediately and starts crying. This is weird; can she sense my feelings so quickly?

I'm scared; I don't know what's going to happen. Dad just stands in the doorway with Miss Tina behind him.

I look past him at Miss Tina, hoping that she'll see the plea on my face... "Please don't leave me alone with him."

I love her when she walks past him towards my bed, taking Monday from me, and says, "Here, meet your granddaughter."

He steps forward and looks at Monday, who's crying. Nothing stops her, and Miss Tina gives her back to me. I hold her tight and talk into her ear, louder than she's crying so that she'll listen to me, and I pat her butt fast to get her attention. She stops crying and shakes her head from side to side with her mouth open. She's as stressed as I am, and I do the only thing I know will comfort her. I pull my shirt open and, even though my dad's watching, and any other time I'd have been mortified to let him see my breast, I pull Monday towards me.

She latches on to me immediately and is quiet. I feel my own heartbeat slow and we feel as if we're one.

"Do you want me to stay?" Miss Tina asks.

I'm determined to be honest with my dad, but I feel scared, so I want her to stay.

"Yes, please."

"Is that okay with you?" she asks my dad.

He seems flustered and nods over and over. "Yes. Yes, of course," he says, and it occurs to me that he sounds different...his voice isn't strong and in control. He sounds weird.

Miss Tina pulls up a chair on either side of my bed, and she winks at me when he can't see. She gives me strength.

"Let's go and get some coffee first," she says to him. "And while I make it, you can read the story Hannah's worked on in group. Do you take sugar?"

They're gone for what seems like ages, and my stomach's in shreds. Monday's asleep again. She wasn't hungry; she just needed to be comforted. I hum in her ear, trying to keep myself calm.

Miss Tina and Dad come back and he sits down awkwardly.

"Well, that was a neat story," he says, clearing his throat. "I guess my feet are wet."

I want to giggle but don't.

Dad's stuck on top of a hill, about to drown, and he doesn't know what to do. I'm standing on another hilltop; he's scared and so am I. I do the only thing I can think of...I need to build a bridge and hope that he will build one to reach mine over our sea of mistrust.

"Would you like to hold her?" I ask, and he immediately stands up and comes to the edge of my bed.

I know that he's just built his part of the bridge, and I feel slightly relieved.

I hand her over to him, and something weird happens to him in the same way that it happened to Zak; he goes all gooey and his eyes glisten.

His face seems shocked, yet soft. I've never seen him this way. He's not the man I know, the one who's constantly finding fault with people and berating their way of life. He seems gentle and vulnerable. I realize that I don't know him at all. He really *is* alone on top of a hill...isolated and afraid.

I feel tears prick my eyes but blink them back instantly. I'm sure he notices, and I'm annoyed with myself.

"She's beautiful. What's her name?"

I hesitate because I know that he'll be expecting a Susan or a Jennifer, but he has to know and I'm prepared to tell him my reasons for her name, so even though I feel nervous, I say, "Her name is Monday."

"Monday?" he frowns, with the same curiosity that I knew he'd show, curiosity tinged with contempt. "Monday? How come you want to call her *Monday*?"

So I tell him. I didn't choose to become pregnant but now that she's here, I can't be without her. I love her so much.

Dad holds her, and he grins when she pokes her tongue out at him. I wish I could poke my tongue out at him and get away with it. He looks at me and then at Miss Tina, and there are tears in his eyes.

"What d'you want to say to your daughter?" Miss Tina asks.

He looks stricken...silenced.

He shrugs, but not in a bad way. He just looks lost.

"I...I don't know." He looks at me, and a tear rolls down his face. I feel wrenched in two. This is my dad; he's always been strong, yet he looks broken. I feel so guilty. I know I have to say something, so I get it over with.

"I'm so sorry I lied to you, Dad, but I was too scared to say anything. I knew that you'd be angry and disappointed in me. You went crazy after I threw up in your car, so I just couldn't bring myself to tell you something that was much more serious."

He looks at me and something twists on his face. My stomach churns and I feel sick.

"You lied to me, Hannah, you know how I can't stand people lying to me. You lied about the party and then lied for *nine* months."

Monday starts to wail and Dad looks perplexed. He shifts her onto his shoulder and starts patting her, but it does no good. Perhaps she can feel that he's upset and his tone of voice has changed.

He pats her back but she won't be pacified. Her cries tear at my heart.

I reach out to him. "Can I have my daughter back, please?"

He stands up and hands Monday back to me. Her cries make him fade into the distance...my fear fades with it. Something's changing in this room and I don't really understand it.

As I put Monday to my breast again, she sucks for just a few seconds and then is asleep, her distress gone. I hold her firmly towards me and decide that I don't want to hand her around for everyone to hold, because it just seems to upset her. Maybe she can sense everyone's feelings and doesn't like it.

I feel whole with her in my arms, and if she could speak, I bet she'd say the same.

When Monday settles, I glance at my dad and Miss Tina. She's smiling, but Dad looks agitated.

"You lied to me for *nine* months," he says, shrugging, like he didn't make his point the first time around and doesn't know what to do with the truth.

"I know, and I really am sorry. I don't know how else to say how sorry I am. I just couldn't tell you."

I feel a sudden sense of strength—I'm a mother now, I'm in charge of another human being, someone who's completely dependent upon me, and that gives me the strength I need to stand up for myself.

"Listen, Dad, I felt so bad on the night of the party," I say. "I was ashamed of myself. I never intended to get drunk, nor did I intend to lie. I don't know why Linda lied to you. She lied for her own reasons; they weren't mine. I know I should have been honest about the party at the time, but I couldn't stand against her because she's my friend. I should have, but I didn't. You're wrong about her. You really hurt her that night, and now she believes that she's in some way responsible for what's happened to me.

"She's not responsible, Dad. I am. I'm responsible for what I did, not Linda. It was Linda who fixed everything for me at school after you went over to Zak's to cause trouble."

I don't dare tell him that Zak was going to mail my panties to him.

"She was there for me during the first few months, so please don't be hateful towards her. You made my life hell at school because you went to Zak's demanding that his parents do something about him."

I want to cry as the anger and injustice pour out of me.

Miss Tina speaks out. "Okay, hold it. It seems to me that you're both feeling hurt. Let's not get bogged down with specific events. Let's talk about how you're both feeling and try to resolve this."

Dad shifts in his seat. I feel strangely deflated, having just vented my anger upon him. I feel a little bit ashamed, too.

"The thing that keeps people connected and close to each other is trust," Miss Tina says, "and we all know that telling lies breaks trust, but we need to examine why a person feels compelled to lie in the first place. Why d'you think that your daughter felt that she had to lie to you, or that she couldn't come to you with something as important as being pregnant?" she asks my dad.

He becomes very quiet and eventually mumbles, "Because she knew I'd be mad."

Miss Tina leans forward and suddenly looks very serious. "It's more than that, though; it's deeper. The point of the story you've just read is that when people don't feel accepted by those around them, they feel compelled to defend themselves by lying, even though lying breaks trust and makes you less likely to feel accepted. So it seems that the key issue here is 'acceptance,' and what I hear from Hannah is that you are not accepting of her, or the fact that she is different than her sister, who possesses the qualities *you* think are important. Does that make any sense to you?"

He nods and looks cornered, yet there's something on his face that looks more like sadness than defensiveness or anger.

"Hannah, I only want what's best for you. Yes, I want to be different from my family and I don't want either of you to end up like them because I know how painful it is. I know how hard life is when you're poor and don't have any support. All I've ever wanted was for you girls to have a better childhood than your mother and I had."

I hear what he's saying, and I've heard it a hundred times before. Although I believe him— because, holding Monday, I want the best for her too—there's more to it than that. I don't feel that he's being really honest with me, so with my new-found honesty I challenge him. I'm so glad Miss Tina's in the room.

"I understand that, Dad, but you seem more concerned with what your families will say about me getting pregnant than about me. Mom told me that you'll be devastated when your family starts to pick on you about your daughter being the same as theirs."

He gets red in the face and starts to stutter.

"I...I...I don't deny that they'll rip me to pieces and I don't look forward to it, but I'll just have to learn to cope with it, I suppose."

He looks sheepish and I suddenly feel sorry for him. It's not his fault that his family is awful. I know how much he and Mom have tried to make a better life for themselves and for us girls. I feel that where he's gone wrong is to brag so much to his family about his successes, trying to make himself feel better and them feel bad.

As I think these things, I realize that this is a lesson for him to learn on *his* life's journey, and it's not mine. I have other lessons to learn but not this one. I've never felt I was better than anyone; I like the fact that we're all different.

Miss Tina looks at him and says, "As far as I can see, the only way to rebuild the trust between you is to understand why each of you thinks the way you do, and then to accept each other unconditionally. If you can both do that and make a pact to be completely honest with each other, then you'll learn to trust each other. Then you'll feel safe knowing that you are totally accepted, even though you may think differently."

I look at him and he looks at me and shakes his head.

He says, "I'm sorry I've been hateful towards Linda. I guess I blamed her because I didn't want to blame you."

My heart hurts as I hear his pain.

"I'm responsible for my mistakes, Dad, not anyone else, not Linda and not Zak."

He becomes very quiet at the mention of Zak's name, and he looks so broken that I don't pursue it. I can't, because suddenly I don't feel angry with him anymore, and why would I want to hurt someone who already looks broken?

"I'm so sorry, Dad, I wanted to tell you time and time again. But I knew that I'd disappoint you so much, and I couldn't face it because I knew that you'd be devastated. I didn't know what to do, and as I kept it secret over the weeks—and they became months—there was never a time when I could tell you, because I'd have to admit that everything about me had been a lie. I couldn't do it, I just couldn't. I wasn't that brave, and then I couldn't see a way out."

I'm irritated with myself because I can feel tears starting to roll down my face and I don't seem to be able to stop them.

"I've never felt so alone and desperate...I couldn't tell anyone, no one, and all I wanted to do was die, but I couldn't even do that because my beliefs wouldn't allow me to kill my baby. I felt like a prisoner. I felt damned. I couldn't live with myself after I'd left Monday on the church steps..."

I'm sobbing as the memory of what I did flows through me, and Monday wakes up and screams. Miss Tina takes her from me, wraps her tight and croons in her ear.

As I hear her crying, I imagine her crying as she was left in my pink sports bag, and my heart feels broken. How could I have done that?

"I couldn't face what I'd done," I sob, "and so I wanted to die...I'm so sorry, Dad."

Dad's crying too, and it turns my stomach to see him in as much pain as I am.

"Hannah, don't you know that you and Jacky are our life? We couldn't live without either of you," he says, his voice croaking. "You mean more to us than anything. I couldn't bear it if anything happened to you. Don't you realize that?"

"But you never said."

He blows his nose and I blow mine.

We're quiet for a moment while the shame that settles on him matches my own.

"I'm sorry," he says, "I didn't know how to show you what you mean to me because I was too busy trying to make sure my family did better than my own brothers and sisters and their families. I'm so sorry, baby."

Monday has stopped yelling and Miss Tina hands her back to me.

"Mom and I want you to come home as soon as possible and we'll help you all we can. Just because you've had a baby doesn't mean that you can't be successful,"—Miss Tina shoots him a look—"in whatever *you* want to do, I mean."

He looks at Miss Tina and says, "I know I've tried to push Hannah to be like Jacky, and I need to accept that my girls are different and may want different things. I'm going to work hard on trying to change."

He looks flustered and uncomfortable.

"Mom and I are going to help you all we can, Hannah, so that you can realize your true potential, whatever that may be," he adds quickly. "And hang my rotten family," he says, with a grin spreading across his face.

"Dad, I promise that I'll never lie to you ever again, even if what I say hurts you, or isn't what you want to hear. Deal?"

He smiles at me and says, "Deal."

Something strange happens; he looks younger, less rigid and stiff, as if he's someone new that I've never met before. I feel like he's invited me into his house on top of a flooded hill so that I can learn about who he really is and what lives in his home, inside him. And I feel an overwhelming sense of love for him.

He comes over to me and puts his arms around me and Monday, and he holds us tight.

"I'm so sorry," he says, and I tell him I'm sorry, too.

"I love you, Dad."

"I love you, too, and I love Monday as well," he says, stroking her cheek.

Miss Tina walks quietly away, closing the door behind her, leaving us to build bridges, and to find out what trust feels like.

# About the Author

Dr. Celia Banting earned her Ph.D. by studying suicide attempts in adolescents and developing a risk assessment tool to identify those young people who may be at risk of attempting suicide. She identified several risk factors which, when combined, could increase the likelihood of an individual attempting suicide. Rather than write "how to" books or text books to help teenagers cope with the risk factors, Dr. Banting has incorporated therapeutic interventions into novels that adolescents will be able to identify with. These novels are designed to increase the adolescents' ability to take care of themselves, should they have minimal support in their families.

Dr. Banting's career has revolved around caring for children in a variety of settings in both the United Kingdom and the United States. She is dedicated to helping troubled children avoid the extreme act of suicide.

# WIGHITA PRESS ORDER FORM

| Book Title | Price | Qty. | Total |
|---|---|---|---|

**I Only Said I Had No Choice**
ISBN 0-9786648-0-9        $14.99  x _____  $_____
 Shane learns how to control his anger and make positive life
 choices; and he gains understanding about adult co-dependency.

**I Only Said "Yes" So That They'd Like Me**
ISBN 0-9786648-1-7        $14.99  x _____  $_____
 Melody learns how to cope with being bullied by the in-crowd
 at school and explores the emotional consequences of casual
 sex. She raises her self-esteem and learns what true beauty is.

**I Only Said I Couldn't Cope**
ISBN 0-9786648-2-5        $14.99  x _____  $_____
 Adam learns how to deal with grief and depression. He works
 through the grieving process and explores his perceptions of
 death and life.

**I Only Said I Didn't Want You Because I Was Terrified**
ISBN 0-9786648-3-3        $14.99  x _____  $_____
 Hannah experiences peer pressure to drink alcohol. She learns
 about teenage pregnancy, birth, and caring for a new baby.
 Hannah faces the consequences of telling lies and learns how to
 repair broken trust.

**I Only Said I Was Telling the Truth**
ISBN 0-9786648-4-1        $14.99  x _____  $_____
 Ruby embarks upon a journey to rid herself of the damaging
 emotional consequences of sexual abuse.

Sub Total  $_____

Sales Tax 7.5% ($1.13 per book)  $_____

Shipping/handling  $_____
1st book, $2.50; each add'l. book $1.00 / U.S. orders only.
(For orders outside the United States, contact Wighita Press.)

**TOTAL DUE**  $_____

PLEASE PRINT ALL INFORMATION.

Customer name: _____

Mailing address: _____

City/State/Zip: _____

Phone Number(s): _____

E-mail address: _____

**Make check or money order payable to Wighita Press and
mail order to:** P.O. Box 30399, Little Rock, Arkansas 72260-0399
Look for us on the web at: www.wighitapress.com   (501) 455-0905